A Girl Made of Dust

NATHALIE ABI-EZZI

A Girl Made of Dust

Grove Press
New York

First Published in Great Britain in 2008 by Fourth Estate,
an imprint of HarperCollins *Publishers*

ISBN-13: 978-8021-1895-0

Grove Press
an imprint of Grove/Atlantic, Inc.
841 Broadway
New York, NY 10003
Distributed by Publishers Group West
www.groveatlantic.com

09 10 11 12   10 9 8 7 6 5 4 3 2 1

For Jeddo

Chapter One

'It's thanks to the *'adra* that you didn't get killed today.' Teta crossed herself, and her lips moved in a silent prayer as we sat on her bed folding clothes that were stiff and bent in strange shapes from the sun.

The room seemed darker and heavier than usual, with its old furniture, and the tired curtains that wanted to lie down if only the hooks would let them. Through the window, the tops of the pine trees dropped into the valley, where white stone buildings stuck out tall from between them like giant fingers; and further down still to Beirut, which lay stretched out beside the sea. The hot sky had bleached itself white and cicadas hummed back and forth, back and forth, as if they were sawing the trees. Teta had said once that each time they stopped a person had died, but they didn't stop often: their throbbing started early in the morning when the light came over the mountains and didn't stop till it went away again.

'I fell all the way down from the ledge. The earth crumbled and it was *so* far, higher than the ceiling.'

'What? Are you a half-wit, Ruba, to be playing in the forest next to a steep fall like that? Are you, girl?' She touched my cheek. 'In any case *she*'s the one who saved you.'

'The Virgin?' I gazed at the little yellow-haired plastic woman in a blue dress standing on the dressing-table. She was really only a bottle filled with holy water that you could see if you unscrewed her crown and I didn't see how she could have saved me that morning.

Teta nodded. 'You could have fallen as far as hell itself and you wouldn't have been killed. The Blessed Virgin wouldn't have let you die.'

'Is that her job? Is that what she does?'

'Does?' Teta gave me a look. 'She's not a belly-dancer, child, she's the Mother of Christ.'

I didn't really want to hear about the Virgin Mary unless Teta put her into a story and made her do something exciting like swim out to sea, or play hide-and-seek with God, or dig a tunnel all the way to Beirut and live in it.

The huge pair of grey-white pants I was trying to fold didn't want to be made small. They were grandmother pants; no one but grandmothers ever wore that sort.

'But she couldn't have saved me because she wasn't even there.'

Teta smiled. 'She was there.'

Maybe Teta was right. Perhaps the Virgin had wanted me to fall; she had *made* me fall so I could find the glass eye.

'If only she'd help your father as well,' Teta murmured.

I looked up from the pants, but she didn't say anything more, just carried on untangling, shaking and folding. A thin green blouse slid out from the pile, was laid flat and smoothed: Teta's hands were slow and heavy, and things obeyed them.

'Does she really look like that?' I pointed at the plastic bottle full of holy water. 'Or like Teta Fadia? Teta Fadia looks

2

like an angel.' A photograph of Teta's mother, wedged into the frame of the dressing-table mirror, showed a woman older than anyone I'd ever seen bent over a walking-stick. Her white hair was parted in the middle and tied back, and she wore a pair of horn-rimmed glasses; but behind them was a kind, soft face.

'She *was* an angel,' said Teta. 'Haven't I told you how it's because of her that I can read? "Why should my sons go to the school and not my daughter?" she used to say. "Aren't I a daughter?" And so my brothers and I took turns to tend the goats and go to school.'

Teta didn't look like her mother. There was still a lot of black in her hair, she was strong with large hips, and her face was neither soft nor beautiful, just round and wrinkled and wonderful.

As I watched her smiling reflection in the mirror folding and stacking, I fingered the glass eye in my pocket. It was hard and dense, and I hadn't told anybody about it.

'Naji will have come back. I'm going to see.' When early afternoon had changed into late afternoon and the shops were reopening, Mami had gone with Naji to buy food and house-things. Only Papi was at home.

Teta's heavy hands shook out a towel. 'Yes. Go and find your brother.'

My shoes squeaked down the tiled floor of the corridor. Light came in through the doors leading onto the large balcony, but the middle of the flat was as quiet and dim as if it was under water. The bulb above the sink in the corridor was switched on, and in the shadows, the sewing-machine with 'Singer' on it was crouched like a black bear. I put up my nose as I passed the bunch of dried lavender

3

that hung from a nail in the wall: it smelt of sleep and open spaces.

Above the wooden double doors, a huge embroidered picture of Christ's head bled and shone out great beams of light, the eyes staring up at the top of the frame so that the whites showed. In the dining room there was another picture of him, only in that one he was eating with a lot of other men. Teta said it was his last supper, but wouldn't say what the food was or where the women who'd prepared it had gone.

The door shivered shut and I headed up the stairs into the white sunshine.

The August sun shone like Jesus, and across the road, large black flies worried the thin dogs and cats that stepped among the rubbish or leapt onto the garbage drums. At midday, sweating shopkeepers pulled down their shutters, went home to have lunch and rest, and the afternoon slump set in. People and plants wilted together; only the pine trees remained upright like soldiers in the heat. Dust rose and settled whenever a car chugged slowly uphill, cats and young women yawned, and the town waited for the shadows to grow long.

I didn't want to be alone in the house with Papi, so I stayed on the veranda that ran three-quarters of the way round the building. Sliding down to the floor, I sat with my back to the wall.

Mami always said that time passed quickly, and maybe it did in other places – in Beirut or on the beach or in the Roman temples at Baalbek that were in our history books at school, or at the top of the snowiest mountain – but here in Ein Douwra, it went slowly. The Rose Man came down the stairs onto the far end of the veranda, smiled at his roses as he walked past them, and carried on up the hill, easing himself from foot to foot, lifting and settling his stick, stopping at every fifth or sixth step to rest and look around. He was slow, and time moved even slower than he did. It had taken for ever to get to 1981, and would take for ever again to reach my eighth birthday.

Finally there was a crunch of gravel and Mami appeared, sweating and red-faced, weighed down with bags of shopping. Naji came behind, carrying two more and stamping his feet in time to a song he was chanting. He followed Mami into the house, and a minute later came back out again. 'What happened to you?' he asked, looking at my cuts.

I turned first one way and then the other to show Naji the best ones.

'What happened?'

'I fell down that ledge in the forest, the steep one.' I pointed the short distance down the slope to where the trees were singing, their chirps stitched together in an endless row. The forest was the best place to be, with its green pine needles and grasses, its brown trunks and rock, its bright coloured flowers, gleaming insects, thorn bushes, and the dry red earth of its narrow paths. 'The skin tore as I slid down. There are still bits of grit in, see?' I poked at the black specks on my knee.

Naji's eyebrows rose as if he didn't believe me.

'I did! I tried to get hold of some roots but I couldn't.'

'What was at the bottom, if you fell?'

'There were all sorts of things – twigs and a rusty can and pine cones.' My fingers still smelt of the young cones that had been all hard and green with a silver diamond on each scale. 'And then I found . . .'

His eyes lit up. 'What?'

'Nothing. When I got back and you and Mami weren't here, I went to Teta's, and she touched me all over to check that every bit of me was still there. It tickled! And there was blood on my shirt from the cut on my shoulder. It looked like a flower – it got bigger . . . like a rose! – and then Teta put spirit on my scratches, which hurt even more than falling over.'

But Naji was two years older than me and wasn't interested in such things. He went inside. When he came back he was carrying a Matchbox car, his bag of marbles and the blue tin box that lived on the top shelf of his bookcase where I couldn't reach. He kept his most precious things in it.

'Teta said it was the Virgin who stopped me dying when I fell.'

He stroked the little white sports car. 'It's a Lamborghini. Look.' He flicked the doors so they opened upwards, then closed them again.

'Do you think it's true, Naji?'

He ran the car quickly across one palm so the wheels whizzed. 'No. The Virgin Mary's not here at all. Didn't you hear how they saw her in a building site in Beirut?'

'Who saw her?'

'Just people. Gabriel's mother told us. She said miracles were happening just twenty kilometres down the road from here in Beirut.'

'But Teta doesn't lie.'

He shrugged.

A rumble of shelling was coming from somewhere as Naji emptied his pockets to see if there was anything precious to add to the box. There was a long piece of string with knots tied in it, his old penknife, a little block of wood with a hole bored through it, a round of caps and some more marbles.

'I've got a marble too,' I said.

Naji's black eyebrows lowered. 'Where is it? When did you get it?'

'Today. I found it.' It was still in my pocket, warm from being against me all afternoon. 'Here!' I plopped it into his hand.

He gasped. The glass eye jumped up and down twice in his palm, and I sat on my heels and laughed.

'Where did you get it?'

I told him how I'd found it in the forest, and he turned the eye over, examining it closely. It looked funny lying in his hand without a body round it, and I thought about people being made up of separate parts – ears and fingers, hair and belly-buttons.

'Do you think it's hers?'

He glanced up. 'Whose?'

'*Hers!*'

He peered more closely, as if it might have her name on it. 'The witch?'

I nodded.

'Probably.'

Ever since we were old enough to think, we'd known she'd put a spell on Papi to make him the way he was.

'I know!' I cried. 'It's the evil eye!'

Naji looked doubtful. 'Maybe.'

'She's probably got more than one so she can swap them round depending who she wants to put the evil eye on. Big eyes for big curses and little ones for smaller curses – a drawer full, all rolling about when she opens it!'

Naji sighed, which meant he didn't think I knew anything. 'There's only one evil eye,' he said, 'but if it is hers she can't put a curse on us because we've got it.' His face lit up. 'Like a miracle. Miracles are always happening.'

'What other miracles happen?'

He put the glass eye to his, maybe to find out if he could see with it. 'Mar Sharbel.'

'What's he ever done?'

'He's our saint and there's always stuff about him, how sick people get better.'

The rumble of shelling that was always in the background came again, carried on the still air. 'How?'

He waved his hand, as if there were too many instances to remember. 'If they're blind they grow new eyes, or new legs if they can't walk.'

But we weren't missing any legs, arms, eyes or even teeth. We were only missing Papi.

Mami talked to herself – made noises, her face twisted or frowning or sad: the slight sucking in of breath when she cut herself, the annoyed '*tut*' when she was rolling up *fatayir* into parcels and the dough wouldn't stick together, the '*ach*' when she straightened up from making beds, the long sigh like the sea when she sat down at the end of the day. She even talked to the chicken when she was preparing it for the oven, sympathetically as if she was sorry. And then there was the sound of her: the rustle of the underskirt against her legs, the clack of her wooden slippers, the tinkling of her two gold bangles, the click of her hips as she shifted from one foot to the other, the tiny *tick* when she bit down on hairpins while coiling her hair.

Papi didn't make these noises. He was as quiet as a stone.

Perhaps Mami liked to cook because the kitchen talked back to her: the bubble and hiss of the pots, the crushing and chopping that came from the board, the clatter and tinkle of knives and glasses, the creak of the table, the whirr of the fridge, and the *tlup-tlup-tlup* of the dripping tap.

Naji must have left footprints when he left to go to Gabriel's because the stretch of kitchen floor between the dining room and the veranda door was newly cleaned and wet. I almost sent a tray crashing to the white-tiled floor.

'Be careful, *ya* Ruba!'

There were trays everywhere – along the counter and gas hob, on top of the fridge, on two chairs Mami had brought in from the dining room – all covered with pastry dough.

'Why are you cooking so many?'

Mami's face was red from the heat as she wiped her hands on a cloth. 'They won't make much in the end.' Sweat had settled on her upper lip, and she wiped it off with a downward sweep of her forefinger.

'Are they all the same?'

She nodded and started to roll out a new square. Then she lifted it onto her knuckles and, elbows spread sideways, stretched it so thin I could see her face through it. Three times it tore and had to be mended, but finally she cut it up and piled layers of dough on top of each other, brushing them with butter and sprinkling nuts as she went. Several ripped, and a ragged ball of useless skin-like pastry grew.

'Here – chop these nice and fine.' Flour smeared her face as she brushed her hair back with her arm.

It was hard to chop the pistachios. One flew up and hit the saint on the calendar that hadn't been turned for two months. Another spun out onto the floor.

'Patience. Patience will extract sugar from a lemon.'

I rolled a nut between my fingers. 'How?'

But she didn't answer. Two trays came out of the oven and two more went in, the layers of filo like dragonfly wings that crackled when I touched them.

Mami wasn't taking any notice. Bent low, she was arranging more pastry on a tray; like that, her hair looked like a giant snail sitting on the back of her head. Then, as I stepped up close, her eyes widened. 'Ruba, what happened?' A loose strand of her hair tickled my cheek as she leant down, her eyes round and black-rimmed. The light from the window showed specks of flour floating next to her ear in the thick heat.

'I fell. It's all right, Teta put spirit on them,' I explained.

She checked me quickly, then carried on working and moving among the jigsaw puzzle of trays. The green of her dress was dark under the armpits, and her arms wobbled in the heat from the oven.

From the living room came the faint *tack-tack-tack* of Papi's worry beads passing through his thumb and finger one by one, again and again and again.

'Mami, why do you cook all the time?'

'It keeps my thoughts busy.'

'Is that why you didn't notice my cuts?'

She looked worried. 'Yes.'

After the cooking came the washing. Then the clothes were hung out on the veranda and Mami watered the fuchsias, marigolds and geraniums set out against the walls. She flickered in and out of the sun as she passed behind the hanging clothes, and water spilt out dark from the bottom of the pots. Mami was good at taking care of things, at making sure they had enough food and water. Thin streams slid across the veranda and into the gutter. They oozed out from the bottom of every pot except for the leaning cactus tied to a pole that stood alone in the corner. Mami didn't like it and kept hoping it would die, but it wouldn't. She didn't want to throw it away yet I knew she didn't want to water it either. Perhaps her heart had dried out and withered in the heat like a fig. For a moment I pictured it, purple and shrunken, inside her chest. 'Mami, when will you water the cactus?'

She glanced over her shoulder. 'I don't know. Soon.'

'How soon?'

The plastic washing-line creaked but there was no answer. She gave the last few drops to the fuchsia, while further along the wall, the earth round the cactus stayed cracked and hard.

Papi watched silently from his armchair as I crossed the living room, his large dark eyes fixed on me; except for them, he didn't move. A woman was singing out of the little radio he kept on the shelf near his chair.

> 'They put up roadblocks,
> They dimmed all the signs,
> They planted cannons,
> They mined the squares.
> Where are you, love?
> After you we became the love that screams.'

I found a book and sat on the sofa. Above my picture of Ali Baba with the forty thieves, Papi's face looked even more square than usual – a big brown square with a funny reddish mark on his forehead like shoe polish that I had always wanted to rub off. And all the time, the *tack-tack-tack* of his worry beads.

The woman was still singing – '*It is the second summer, the moon is broken*' – and Papi was staring at the cuts on my legs.

'I fell, that's all. It didn't hurt much.'

There were black hairs on his arms where the sleeves were rolled up, on the backs of the hands and above each knuckle; and below that, on his toes in their black leather slippers, on the big ones and the smaller ones lined up in a neat row beside them.

'You must be careful.'

'*O love of days, they will come back, Beirut, the days will come back . . .*'

The reddish mark over his eyebrow seemed bigger now. It reminded me of what Soeur Thérèse had said last time she came in to school to teach us about God and the Bible, watching through her glasses with eyes that saw everything, ready to use the telling-off voice that came straight out of her nose. She talked about Cain and Abel, and how the bad brother had a mark on his head.

In the vase on the table the plastic flowers were dusty, and the smell of burnt pastry hung in the air. Papi had turned into a statue with its eyes fixed on the floor. When he lifted his head again he seemed surprised that I was still there. As I left, it came to me that he was like the cactus. He sat in the corner all hard and dry, as though someone had forgotten to water him.

Chapter Two

The following Sunday, Mami tried to hurry Naji. As we waited for him, she undid her hair and re-coiled it, but it must still have been wrong because she frowned and did it again. 'Nabeel,' she said finally, to Papi, 'won't you come to church with us?'

Papi was still eating his breakfast. 'Don't bring up religion, Aida.'

'For my sake, Nabeel.'

'I have no wish to see people and be stared at by them. To appear in church for the first time in years, like a fool.'

'No one will look. And what do you care if they do?'

Naji's Sunday shoes clacked down the corridor.

'Do what you want, that's between you and your God, but there's no place for me in a church.' He cut a piece of cheese and wrapped some bread round it. The cicadas in the valley throbbed on and on like blood pumping round an aching head.

We went ahead of Mami and Teta. Outside, dust lay over everything. Cars passed, their engines noisy, their tyres sticking to the hot tarmac and squeaking round corners.

Across the road from the church, a man was carrying crates of fruit and vegetables out of a dark store and setting them down in front: huge red apples and tomatoes, bananas, apricots, flashing pink pomegranates, hills of okra, beans and lettuce, while inside big bags of round flatbreads hung from hooks that shone as they caught the light.

'Papi used to come to church,' said Naji.

'When?' I asked, fingering the glass eye in my pocket; I'd decided always to carry it for protection.

'Before. But everything was different then. Remember Jamila who used to cook for us?'

'A little. She was soft and hot when she carried me, and her neck always smelt of parsley . . . and tiny balls of water popped out along her head where her hair started.' I saw again the long cloth wrapped round Jamila's head and the long, thin black plait snaking down her back. 'Did she make nice things?'

'Nicer than Mami's food,' he whispered, '*and* she played with us.'

'Why did she go?'

'Because of Papi. It was when he stopped working and we didn't have enough money. When she had to leave she cried, and kissed us so hard it hurt.' He made smacking noises with his lips. 'That's when Mami first started cooking.'

'I remember.' After Jamila left the house, Mami had stood alone in the middle of the kitchen squeezing her hands. It was around the time that she'd stopped going out so much. That was when the curse had begun. 'The witch is still setting curses,' I said. 'The last time she went into the nut shop, they had a whole batch of bad ones. Ali said he'd never seen it happen that way before.'

'Let's go and ask him,' decided Naji, and we crossed the road and walked along it. My fingers touched everything on the way: rough leaves covered with the smallest white hairs, flowers that grew out of cracks in a wall, the ledge of the local shrine, the hot dusty bonnet of a car, a rough stone wall and, finally, the cool sharpness of peeling paint on metal railings.

The shutters of Papi's shop were closed, and inside everything would be in the dark – the pots and frying-pans, glasses and knives, step-ladders and cloths, plates and smiling porcelain statues, some of which had been standing in the same place for years.

As we went past, Naji gave the metal shutters an angry kick, but he brightened as we stopped in front of the nut shop. 'If only Ali owned it,' he said. 'he'd always give us things.'

The brilliant colours of sweets, chocolates and drinks made it the prettiest place in town. Naji sniffed the smell of hot nuts that drifted out before he called up to Ali. A moment later Ali appeared behind a metal grille above the door in his white cotton vest, looking out as if it was the first time he'd ever seen the world.

'It must be so hot up there,' I called. 'You're soaked in sweat!'

He waved. His round face was gleaming, the left eye pointing slightly outwards, the wide mouth a solid, straight line. 'There's no one but me to roast the nuts. It's hot for them and it's hot for me: they're roasted and I'm roasted!' He laughed at his joke and repeated it to himself.

'Isn't it true about the nuts, Ali?' I shaded my eyes. 'Isn't it true the nuts got spoilt when the witch came in?'

Ali nodded, eyes widening in fear. His hands were caked with salt, his face red from the heat of the fire. 'Couldn't sell them. A whole batch.' He shook his head sadly.

'How did she spoil them?'

'He wouldn't know that,' said Naji. 'I don't know what he thinks about, but not about such things.'

'Ali,' I called, 'what do you think about up there?'

Ali smiled. 'Up here I can see everything so I think about everything.' He vanished, then reappeared and threw down some sugared almonds for us to catch. Two purple ones came my way: he knew I liked the purple ones best.

We stood beside the church, gazing down at the terraces of olive and almond trees. Naji said the Phoenicians made them, but when I asked who they were, he wasn't sure. Below and further away, Beirut lay spread out along the coast like grey and white Lego, the sea glinting beside it.

A queue of traffic formed. A driver had stopped to speak to someone in the road. There was more hooting, and things shouted about one man's sister and another's mother.

Mami and Teta had finally made it up the hill. Teta, in her best black, was huffing to catch her breath. 'It's proof to God that I'm devoted, an old woman like me climbing all this way,' she muttered as she went slowly up the church steps.

It was warm and dim inside. The stone floors were lined with wooden pews in the main part of the church, while chairs were set out in rows down the left and right sides. The tall stained-glass saints looked hot and red-faced in the brilliant light that shone through them and fell on the congregation, making pale outfits glow pink and blue like cartoons. The pews were filled with stiff suits and gold jewellery, the air thick with cologne.

16

We sat near the aisle, Teta and Naji in front of me and Mami. Beside me was a fat lady with a clinky bracelet and a man with a fleshy roll of neck.

'Sit quietly,' whispered Mami to Naji, who was humming and knocking his heel against the pew.

A priest in black robes and a puffed-up hat stood at the pulpit. Like all priests, he had a long beard he chanted through. Then it was our turn and the grown-ups chanted back to him.

Naji glanced back and rolled his eyes, but I was trying to guess when Mami would bow her head, and when the priest would turn round to speak to the altar and the big gold cross again instead of to us. He spoke a foreign language a lot of the time, maybe so God could understand, only I didn't think God would be interested if He'd heard the same thing every Sunday for a hundred years.

The lilies and carnations near the altar were wilting, and the pages of the Bible belonging to the lady next to me stuck sweatily together. Up on the right, a stained-glass saint looked like Uncle Wadih, except that Uncle didn't wear a long cloak. Or blush.

It seemed Mami and Teta had plenty to pray for. They knelt on the cushions with their eyes closed and their lips moving while the priest walked about swinging incense in a container he held by gold chains.

I heard Teta begging God and Jesus to keep a long list of our relatives safe and to bless the souls of her husband and mother. Most of all, though, she wanted 'the children and my sons and daughter-in-law to be happy'. I didn't think God had much work to do with Uncle Wadih, though, because he was always happy.

Mami was praying too. 'Give him back to us. Oh, Allah, please make Nabeel come back to us.'

I prayed too: that the curse on Papi would be lifted, that Uncle would come in time for my birthday, and that I would never have to wear grandmother pants like Teta's.

Outside again, I could almost hear the sun beating down. The men took off their jackets and stood in groups smoking and talking while the women crossed the road to the nut shop to buy boxes of chocolate for Sunday visitors. One gave money to the man in the wheelchair who was always waiting near the steps after church. He had a pair of tattered boots at the ends of his shrivelled legs, and crutches laid across his knees.

'How did the priest swing that incense so high without any falling out? It was over his head.'

'He does that so that God can hear our prayers,' said Teta. 'So they go up to heaven with the smoke.'

They went on ahead.

'The Rose Man says it's no use,' I told Naji, 'that we're like plants – we're here and then we're not. Why do people go to church anyway?'

'I don't know. Perhaps they want something from God. That's when most people go and pray. The rest of the time they don't care much about it.'

The leaves hung loose on the trees, and white morning glories spilt down a wall.

'What does Mami want, then?' I thought of her hardened, dried-up fig heart.

'To be rich, probably. That's what everyone wants.'

But I hadn't heard her pray about that. 'Doesn't God get annoyed because people only go there for Him to fix things that are wrong, the same way they go to a doctor when they're ill?'

He left a wavy finger line along the side of a dusty car. 'Well, He'd be annoyed if you bothered Him when everything was fine, wouldn't He?'

'Taste this.' Mami held something in either hand between thumb and fingertip for each of us to taste. It looked like a piece of stuffed meatball, or it might have been fried cauliflower.

Once it was in my mouth I didn't want to swallow it, but Naji was good at lying about the things that came from Mami's hands.

'Mm.' He smiled, then hurried away.

Mami pounded meat using a stick with a wooden block at the end. She hit the thin piece of meat so hard and for so long that the animal must have hurt even though it was dead. A warm sweet smell of frying onions and pine nuts came from the large bent pan, and a soft *khrish-khrish-khrish* from the wooden board where she was chopping parsley. Her green-specked fingers stopped as she glanced up at the petunias on the window-ledge.

'Why do flowers die in winter?' I asked.

'Because it's too cold.'

She'd put them there to have something pretty to look at, and now I wondered how she would feel when they died.

Naji and I ate enough lunch to stop being hungry, then pushed the food round our plates. Something was bitter, although Papi didn't seem to notice: he just ate at a steady pace with plenty of salt.

Mami was pleading with him to open the shop the next day. 'School's starting soon and we need money. I haven't much left.'

The lines in Papi's face deepened.

'You haven't opened for a week now. Must I go up there again?'

He continued eating, staring at his plate as he chewed.

The rice shook on Mami's fork. A few grains fell off. Maybe Naji had been right and it *was* being poor that was making Mami unhappy.

Papi spoke quietly. 'I'll open the shop. But not tomorrow.'

'When, then? The day after it'll be the same thing.' No one was eating now. 'You'll go back to that chair and not get up.' She put a hand to her forehead. 'You'll sit in that chair and—'

Papi's fork clattered onto his plate. 'What do you want me to do, my love? Go out there and chit-chat with whoever walks in – about nothing? About *nothing*!'

'You don't have to talk to them. No one's asking you to have a conversation.'

'No, just to behave like nothing ever happened. Like this country's not hell! Can't you understand, Aida?'

'No – no! I don't understand how you think we're going to live. Time is passing, the children are growing up, and still . . .' Her hand slid down to cover her eyes.

'Still nothing changes. But am I going to let you all starve? Is that what you think?' Roughly, he pushed away his plate. 'I'll do it, didn't I say so? Just not tomorrow.'

'How are the children going to learn with no books, and how are they to go to school with no clothes or bags or pens?'

She was breathing hard. 'Why can't you . . . ?'

Papi smiled bitterly. 'Have you lost patience with me, *ya* Aida, you, with your bottomless well of patience? You might have to be patient for ever. Do you understand? For ever.'

Mami's lips disappeared into her mouth and she got up.

'Don't bother her,' Naji said to me after lunch, but it was hard not to watch. She must have cleaned every tile in the kitchen: every white one, every blue one, and the ugly spaces where there were no tiles any longer. She had to know every wall and surface and crack in the house, I thought, as I hopped around on one foot. She must know the tassels at the edges of the living-room carpet, which was really an island you couldn't step off barefoot or you'd fall into the cold sea of tiles; she must know the swirls in the peach-coloured lampshade, which looked like a shell and which she said came from Manila but was really from a shop on the high road, only no one wanted to tell her; and she must know that the metal coat hook on the wall was bent from the weight of Papi's heavy winter coat.

I lay on the bedroom floor reading while she swept the veranda. The scratch of the thick straw came through the window, a strong steady brushing except when she stopped to rest. I'd nearly finished the book when the singing started. It wasn't often that she sang, only occasionally when she was alone and thought no one could hear.

I lay there listening to her. The brushing slowed to the speed of her song and blended into it. In the high parts, her voice was clear and wavered, but when she sang low, it came out rough and grainy as sand. It was a beautiful voice, and she was like a princess going round and round sweeping – round and round until one day something wonderful would happen, and then she'd sing all the time.

I sat against Mami that evening and watched her sew holes shut. In his chair on the other side of the room, Papi was staring at one spot, the muscles in his neck tightened into ropes. His head hung low, while his fingers pulled the large green worry beads along, as if they were an endless abacus.

Pulling the sewing basket onto my lap, I busied myself with the different-coloured spools, loose pins, saved patches, zips and worn measuring-tape. I emptied the babyfood jar full of buttons into the lid. There were large flat gold ones, shiny red ones, little carved white ones, warm leather ones – dozens of different colours and sizes.

'Where did they come from?' I picked up a blue button that shone silver when it was tipped in the light.

Mami cut a thread with her teeth. 'That one was Naji's, a costume he wore in his first school play.' She smiled. 'He didn't want to go.'

Naji glanced up from the floor where he sat with his books spread out round him, then something on the television caught his attention.

'And this one?' I picked up a carved white one that felt like bone.

She twirled a thread tight on the spool. 'It's from a dress I wore before we were married, when I was' – she stopped for a moment – 'when I was young.'

I saw Papi twitch as though a mosquito had landed on his cheek, but his eyes didn't move from the carpet.

'Do you remember all the buttons?'

She nodded. 'Most of them. Look, this one's yours.' She pushed a small red one out of the pile. 'One of your first outfits when you were little.'

'Are the big ones Papi's?'

'Some of them.'

'Which ones?'

She started straightening the spools in the basket. 'Never mind now.' The wooden reels tapped softly against each other and the pins wedged into them gleamed secretly among the coloured rolls.

I yawned. 'Why do you keep them when the clothes are gone?'

'I never throw anything away without taking a button off it first. They're memories – each one is like a photo.'

I settled into Mami again, her breast soft and warm against my head, the scent of her a touch vinegary, and sifted her memories through my fingers. They fell with small, hard *tick*s and *clack*s onto the lid. I watched them sleepily: their shine, their holes, their dips and textures. I imagined her head filled with coloured buttons, and suddenly she was walking round and round inside each one, sweeping and crying. Very occasionally she would sing, and her pockets were full of dead yellow petunias.

When I opened my eyes again the room felt different. Naji wasn't there and neither was Mami's warm shoulder. She was on the other side of the room, squatting next to Papi's chair. The television was turned low.

'How can I carry on this way, Nabeel?'

'None of us wants to. Ask anyone,' he replied.

'But darling, time is passing and it won't come again.

Won't you just try, *ha*?' Slowly, she slid a hand onto his arm. 'Please.'

Something seemed to swell in him, rose into his mouth and was swallowed down again.

Mami knelt now, her bare feet disappearing beneath her skirt. 'Please, Nabeel.'

The knuckles of Papi's hand turned into white pebbles. His fist banged the armrest.

Mami pushed herself up. '*Don't* try, then. Just sit here and do nothing!' Her underskirt rustled against her legs. 'You might as well be dead!' She swished past, and as she went, I saw she was crying.

Chapter Three

Amal was the first to arrive. She was a long-limbed girl in an orange coat who had just started at school. No one knew where she'd come from or why. We only knew that she couldn't talk. At school she had to write everything down.

'Go and speak to her,' Teta insisted, giving me a push, but I wouldn't. I'd only invited her to be polite. She wasn't my friend. She wasn't anybody's friend. At school she always sat alone. Not even the teachers knew how to treat her; some were sugary-nice, others ignored her.

Amal put her present on the table and, still wearing her coat, went to sit near the window. Dark hair hung to her shoulders, and her fringe needed trimming. But then, everything about her was a little too long: her legs and neck, her arms and fingers. When she turned to look at me, though, I decided it was her eyes I liked least. They were eyes that made me feel guilty.

Half an hour later she was still sitting at the window. Two boys beside her were screaming with laughter, jumping up and down, but she sat quietly as if they weren't there, playing with a button on her cuff.

'Maybe she *can* speak,' whispered Naji in my ear. 'She might be pretending.'

'Why would she do that? It's a silly thing to pretend.'

He said we could find out. He would step on Amal's foot by mistake and see if she yelped. I watched as he went over and trod casually on it, then strolled back.

'No,' he said. 'She can't speak.'

After I'd blown out the candles, played some party games, and Teta had encouraged Naji and me to eat some more, because we didn't eat enough to keep a bird alive, the Rose Man, who lived upstairs with his two daughters, came in to give me a rose. 'For your birthday, little girl,' he said. He always called us 'little girl' and 'little boy' – Naji said it was because he couldn't remember names.

I thanked him. He often smiled at his bed of rosebushes out on the veranda or touched them as he watered, but I'd never known him pick one before now. He joined Papi in the kitchen, and by the time I went in to put my rose in water, they were deep in conversation, as usual about 'the events'.

'Which army should we prefer?' Papi was saying. 'On one side we have the Palestinian troublemakers, and on the other the Israelis come to remove the problem.' The red stain on his forehead was wrinkled, like a healing burn. 'So long as they give us back Beirut, let them come.'

'Yes, let them come to remove one problem and put ten in its place,' replied the Rose Man sharply. 'There'll be no end that way – none that we want anyway. Blame them if you like – every Christian does, I know – but—'

'So, are we to let them overrun our country?' interrupted Papi. It was always this way, with Papi blaming the Palestinians.

I noticed that even the hair on the Rose Man's chest was white: it stuck up over his shirt, like the hairs on a corncob. He said there was nowhere else for the Palestinians to go, and that in any case they and the Muslim militias were controlled by Syria.

But Papi was coiled tight as a spring. The Palestinians attacked northern Israel, he said, and the reply always came back ten times as strong, and always aimed at civilians. We were stuck in the middle, watching our own people being killed. 'So now let Israel fix it. Let them do whatever they can to get rid of the Palestinians. They're taking over our country like rats.'

'Nabeel,' tutted the Rose Man.

'Like rats, I said,' he repeated. 'They've set up a state in Lebanon the same as they tried to do in Jordan.'

'You're unreasonable, Nabeel. So much hate. Too much.' And I wondered as I left the kitchen why Papi hated the Palestinians so bitterly.

It was busy in the living room, and when Mami told me to take my presents to my room, Karim followed me. Although he was in my class, I didn't really know him and, besides, everyone thought he was weird. Earlier, his light blue suit had made Naji goggle. 'And look at his hair,' Naji had hissed. 'It's been stuck down with glue!' But his present had been ping-pong bats. There was no ball and we didn't have a table, but Naji's whistle had told me he thought it was the best present too.

'I want to be an astronaut.' Standing in my room twisting his neck round uncomfortably in his collar, Karim announced it as though I'd asked him a question. 'I want to fly and wear a helmet and grow five centimetres taller, because you grow five centimetres taller in space.'

27

When I admitted grudgingly that they were good reasons, a crescent moon smile opened in his face, and I saw he'd recently lost a front tooth.

'If you were standing on Mars and looked up, the sky would be pink.'

'How could it be pink?' Pink. A pink sky. Maybe it changed colour every day so it was always a surprise when you woke up. Everything else would be different too: trees would grow sideways and shed feathers instead of leaves, the wind would tell you secrets as it blew, roses would grow big as houses, and there would be no war.

'How come your father's sitting in the kitchen? Doesn't he like children?'

'It's not that. He's just different from other people because he had a curse put on him. He wasn't always like this,' I explained. 'He used to be happy and laugh.' Then I told him how I'd gone up to the witch's house with Naji that summer. 'And we were so close we could see the broken fountain outside.'

Karim's eyes were wide. His hair was unfurling from his head, and his ears stuck out like handles.

'How are you going to go up into space in a giant firework if you're scared of an old witch?' I asked.

'I'm not scared!'

'Okay.' I stood up. 'But everyone thinks you're weird.'

He didn't say anything, and I felt sorry to have said it. Besides, I was starting to like him.

'Where do you live?'

'Up the hill.'

'Do you want to come over and play ping-pong sometime?'

He frowned. 'Do *you* think I'm weird?'

I shrugged. 'Maybe. But you can come anyway.'

We went back into the living room to rejoin the others, and were in the middle of Musical Chairs when the Rose Man left. Behind him, Papi's face was taut. 'All this noise!' he barked. 'Can't you shut up for five minutes?'

The laughter faded. No one spoke, only the music played on.

Teta went up to Papi. 'Son, they're children. It's Ruba's birthday. Let them enjoy themselves.'

'My head's throbbing, and all I can hear is their shouting and squealing. Haven't they had enough yet?'

Teta tried to soothe him, but he swung round to face us. 'That's enough, do you hear? Enough!'

Mami switched off the music. One of the girls had begun to cry.

'All right, son, all right,' said Teta. 'We'll send them home.'

Mami stood staring, her hand still on the radio. Teta was gathering the party bags to give out as everyone left. My birthday was over.

Bursting into tears, I ran out of the living room – past Papi and the remainder of my cake, past the Rose Man's present in its glass of water, and through the kitchen door. My face was hot with crying, but at the bottom of the hill the forest was cool.

The dry stony paths rose and fell to follow the side of the valley. A fistful of devil's snot floated past, thin wisps of cobweb carried on the breeze, white scratches against a blue sky, and then I was under cover.

There must have been a thousand pine trees, and rock-roses and large anemones that made splashes of colour among the thorny bushes. A centipede wriggled under a stone as I passed, a butterfly flashed yellow, and I heard a thousand buzzes, whirrs, chirps and rustles. Beneath that though was a silence deeper than the one in church. Here time stopped and the world went away.

I crouched. An ant climbed over my sandal, over my toes and back onto the ground. A tear dripped into the dust.

A giant moth with an eye on each wing landed on a rock beside me. I watched it open and close its wings. It was like blinking, as if it was looking at me. I put out a finger to touch the large wing-eye but the moth fluttered away.

Then something made me look up. Amal was watching me, her arms wrapped round a thin tree-trunk. There was that questioning look on her face that she often wore, as though everything were a puzzle.

'What do you want?' I screamed. 'Go away!' But she didn't.

I couldn't stop my sobs, so I covered my face to shut her out. The light glowed pinkly through my hands, and all around, I knew it even though I couldn't see them, hundreds of brown eyes peered at me from between leaves, from holes in tree-trunks, from behind rocks.

At last I stood up. 'What do you want?' I yelled. 'Stop spying and go away!'

Amal's arms fell to her sides. She stared, and for an instant I had the strangest feeling, as though I'd cut her. But before I could say more, she turned and left.

Later, when Naji came to find me, I asked him if he remembered when Papi was happy.

He nodded. Mottled light fell through the branches, and somewhere a bird was singing. 'You were five.'

'Tell me.'

He bent down to pick up a stone and started to scratch

vertical lines in the earth. The stone spattered a fine cloud of dust onto his shoe. 'He came back from Beirut one day—'

'Wasn't I there?'

'Yes, but you were little – that's why you can't remember. He came back, and someone was crying.'

'Who? Mami?'

Naji had turned gloomy. 'I don't know. Maybe. There was shouting too.' He stopped and scratched at one of the lines until it stood out. Then he gave it a head, arms and legs.

'What happened after that?'

The pale ghost-head grew thick and heavy as Naji's stone worked round and round.

'You started crying and Teta took you away.'

'Didn't she take you too?'

'No. I stayed.'

He stared at the ground, examining his work: the head, which was thick with lines, was too big and stood out more than the rest of the man.

'Nothing happened for a long time, no sound, no one moving, as if no one was in the house. They didn't come to me for ages – hours, maybe.'

I pictured him sitting on his bed all alone, with no one, not even me: the light faded, his stomach made noises from hunger, his lips turned dry, the room grew blue with evening and still he sat.

Naji carried on drawing lines – two with a roof on them, and suddenly there was a house round the man with the heavy head.

'But what was it that made Papi go that way?'

The scratching stopped and the stone fell from Naji's hand. 'I don't know. I don't know what happened.'

31

Chapter Four

'You children, wasn't your uncle a friend of the departed?' asked the nut-shop owner. He and another man with a bushy moustache had been talking about a funeral while Naji and I chose sweets.

'I'm not sure,' replied Naji.

'Does he mean Uncle Wadih?' I asked. It was the first time Uncle Wadih's name had ever been connected with something bad.

Naji frowned at me. 'He's the only uncle we have, isn't he?'

The shop owner turned back. 'I think the departed had business dealings with Wadih Khouri. Anyway, his wife has family. They'll help her sort out his affairs. Not like my neighbour – her son was killed last week, her only son, and she'd already lost her husband. Now she has no one.'

The customer laid his hands flat on the counter. I noticed the long nail on his little finger, which I thought was for picking his nose but Naji said was to show he wasn't a manual worker. 'The young Mansoor boy? What happened to him?'

'What happened to him, my brother? What happens to any of them? He joined a militia, they picked a fight with some boys from the Lebanese Army and he was sprayed with bullets. When they're young' – the shop owner tapped the side of his head – 'when they're young they don't think.'

The nut shop was lined with containers full of different sorts of sweets, biscuits and lollipops, while shelves along the back wall displayed large boxes of chocolates, most with pictures of green hills, lakes and cows on the front. Ali was humming and roasting upstairs, and behind the glass counter the *bzoorat* were separated by type: watermelon and pumpkin seeds, pistachios, almonds, hazelnuts, cashews, peanuts, in their shells and out, roasted maize, and chickpeas coated with sugar. We were still deciding what to buy.

'Did Uncle really know a dead man?' I asked Naji, but he shushed me. He was listening.

'We could barely lift him,' the customer was saying. 'If his wife hadn't been such a good cook yesterday, maybe I wouldn't have such a bad back today. I'm telling you, a crane would have found it difficult to lift him. Don't think badly of me, I don't wish to speak ill of the dead, and I loved the man, but there was too much of him for his own sake as well as mine.' He rolled his moustache between thumb and forefinger. 'My spine was creaking the whole way – and his wife had her eye on us from start to finish.'

Naji's elbow poked me in the ribs. 'They're talking about that funeral – the one when we had to get off the bus.' Some days ago the street had been black with mourners, inching their way to the church like a stream of melting tar so that we'd had to get off our school bus and walk. Women in the crowd had wailed, a pair of hands rising occasionally to the sky. And at the head of all this the coffin had moved silently along, like a boat with no sail.

As we left, grey clouds were gathering on the horizon like dirty soapsuds. Autumn was coming. The leaves were turning yellow, and humidity built up during the day until steam rose from the sea in the afternoons that made the air thick and rubbed out Beirut so that only its ghost-lines were left. In the evenings people sat out on their balconies less often, closed their shutters at night, and Mami had climbed into the attic to bring down clothes that smelt of mothballs. And behind everything, the growl of shelling had become insistent.

When we got home, Papi was reading his newspaper and the telephone was ringing.

Mami answered. 'Yes, I . . . I'm well. We're all well.' Her free hand went to her hair first, then to her skirt, slipped to the edge of the dresser, then hooked onto the phone cord. She glanced at Papi and his paper sank to his lap.

There was a little more talk, then Mami stopped moving, her fingers strangled in the coiled cord. 'Of course.' Her voice didn't change, it was still polite and cool, only her hand closed into a fist that made the cord quiver.

After she'd put down the phone she stood quite still, and the black kohl that she pencilled round her eyes in the morning made them seem enormous now. Slowly, she unwound the phone cord from her fingers. 'It was Wadih.'

Papi looked at the phone, then back at her. 'Why didn't he speak to me?'

'I don't know.' Her feet shuffled uncomfortably. 'He's coming over.'

'Uncle Wadih's coming?' yelled Naji.

Papi moved to the edge of his seat. 'Coming here? When?'

'Today.'

Papi got to his feet. 'Has something happened?'

'No, nothing. All he said was he's coming. You know how he is. That's just his way.' She frowned and laid a hand on top of her head, as if to stop it flying off. 'And now I have even more to do.'

'But what did he say?'

'Didn't you hear me? Nothing!' She clicked her tongue in annoyance.

The nut-shop owner had asked us about Uncle Wadih not half an hour ago, and now he was coming.

Naji and I didn't know what to do with ourselves. The hands of the clock in the dining room refused to move round as fast as they usually did, and we grew jumpy as two fleas. The walls felt too close, the ceiling too low, and the smell of cooking too heavy. Mami's sighs and tuts fluttered through the stillness like moths, and even though no sweat droplets formed on her upper lip, her cheeks burnt redder and redder.

'That's him!' Naji cried each time he heard a car, but every time it carried on past.

'When will he come?' I asked Mami for the hundredth time. 'Is he going to stay?'

She didn't answer, so I tried again.

'Don't pester me about your uncle,' she snapped, so we went outside to wait.

Beneath the darkening sky, a strange cotton-wool quiet had fallen.

'When was the last time he came, Naji?'

'Maybe two years ago, or three. He used to come more often – he used to come all the time.'

'Why did he stop?'

'Maybe . . .' Naji hesitated. 'He was here the day it happened, the day I was telling you about.'

I hopped off the gate. 'Let's go and tell Teta.'

Standing in the doorway with Jesus's sun-head blazing above her, Teta smiled, laughed. Her eyes almost cried. A minute later she hurried across the road to our house, her bare heels peeling off her slippers with each step, *shlup-shlup-shlup* through the still air. And a little before one o'clock, a shiny cream Mercedes pulled up underneath the large fig tree across the road.

Plenty of old, dusty brown Mercedes passed up and down the hill during the day, their exhaust pipes exploding every now and then, their rears hanging low to the ground, but this one was new and gleamed, like a sucked sweet.

The man who stepped out of it looked as though he'd been polished too. For a moment I was nervous, but then he held out his arms. 'Is this pretty young lady my niece?' He laughed, lifting me up to kiss me.

His neck smelt of hot wood and brown spices, and his pale yellow jacket was crisp against my arms. When he put me down, I couldn't help asking, 'Weren't you taller before?'

'No, stupid,' said Naji, 'you were smaller.' For that he got a slap on the shoulder and a ruffle of the hair, something that would usually have annoyed him, only today he didn't seem to mind.

'*Yalla*, let's go and see your parents.'

It was only then that I looked properly at Uncle Wadih. He had heavy-lidded eyes, a sleek, well-fed air that made me think of a rabbit, and his shoes were mirror-clean. We jogged on ahead of him, and when I glanced back I noticed how calm he seemed, how there was a neat line down the front of

36

each trouser leg, and how he moved at the same pace the whole time, like mercury.

Teta was waiting. She disappeared into his chest and came out with wet eyes, her face squashed in joy. Then Mami came out. She had on her best shirt, a brown silk one with pink trimming along the neck and waist – a shirt that usually hung in the back of her wardrobe, but was hardly ever worn. She mustn't have wanted Uncle to crease it because when he reached out, she took a step backwards. In the end, though, he laid a hand on each of her arms and they kissed three times on both cheeks, as adults did.

'How are you, my brother?' Uncle beamed as Papi came forward, and the brothers hugged each other hard the way Naji and I did when we fought. When they drew apart, Papi's face seemed tauter and younger. 'Did you think you'd got rid of me?' Uncle asked as we stepped indoors.

'Don't joke, Wadih,' replied Papi. 'They're fighting all round your building down there, and still you don't come up.'

Naji stopped in his tracks and shot me a look as Uncle settled himself into Papi's chair.

Papi hesitated, but a moment later sat down on the sofa. 'Tell us what's been happening. What's your news?'

'What can I tell you?' Uncle shrugged. 'Life continues as always, only worse.' He gazed round the room – at the old sofa, the table with its tray of cigarettes, the vase of plastic flowers, the wall with its single picture of a small boat far out to sea. And Mami sucked her bottom lip and lowered her flushed face to examine her fingernails.

Naji and I helped to carry Uncle's two cases to Teta's and watched him unpack. One case was full of clothes, perfectly folded, which he removed and smoothed out with his long hands before hanging them up in the empty old wardrobe. The clinking of the spare metal hangers sounded like bells as he closed the door and turned to the second, heavier, case that still lay on the candlewick bedcover. When he opened it there was nothing inside but books, written in Arabic, French and English.

'Are they all poetry?' asked Naji, flicking through one with his thumb.

'Not all. Some are plays, some philosophy.'

'What's this one?' I picked up a book with dozens of naked figures on its cover, all crammed so close together that they were nearly falling off the page. Some were tied and injured. Others pushed boulders up slopes or struggled out of coffins or drowned in blood. And everyone in that strange, cruel place was trying to get out. I looked to see if snipers were shooting from the top of a building anywhere.

Uncle glanced over. 'You see those people? They're in hell.'

I studied it more closely. 'Is that what hell looks like?'

He shrugged. 'No, maybe not.'

We went back to our house for lunch. It was true that Mami's cooking had improved lately: there was boiled chicken with rice and nuts, stuffed aubergines and a dish of *hummus* as well. When she finally carried in the rice, though, it smelt burnt.

Papi brought out the bottle of *arak* and poured a little for himself and Uncle, then added some water so the clear liquid turned to a thin milk. After the first sip, the aniseed scent came light on his breath.

Teta watched each mouthful of food Uncle took. 'I don't know what you eat down there in Beirut,' she muttered.

'I don't know who cooks for you or looks after you,' but Uncle only smiled. As he ate, he moved as though his joints were well oiled.

When he was full, he wiped his mouth and fingers carefully with a napkin, leant forward to let out a soft belch, then sat back. 'What's all this cooking? Are you trying to make us fat?'

Mami turned red and started clearing up. Papi never said anything about a meal, whether it was good or bad.

'Her touch is good for food,' said Teta, smiling.

Mami shook her head. 'The rice was burnt and the chicken was tough. The *hummus* had too much lemon in it.'

Uncle tutted. 'We don't give compliments easily, do we, my mother? And it is a compliment. A mean person can't cook well. You have to have a big heart, a generous hand and an honest eye to make good food.'

Mami stopped, holding a bunch of knives and forks like flowers, and her face was suddenly full of light. Perhaps her shrunken fig-heart was swelling again.

We moved to the sofa, and I inspected Uncle Wadih. He looked younger than Papi, even though he wasn't. Teta said there were three years between them, yet it was Papi's hair that was greying, his face that was pulled in all the wrong directions, and his eyes that seemed to see everything and nothing. Uncle had slick black hair and an unlined, easy face.

'This uncle of yours,' said Papi, looking happy, 'you see his shiny car out there? Well, the summer he bought his first banged-up one, we used to go down to Beirut in it. You remember, Wadih, how you used to drive slowly and not let me roll down any of the windows? The temperature was in the thirties, the sweat pouring off us, and still you wouldn't open them.'

'Why not?' asked Naji.

Papi smiled. 'So the girls would think his car had air-conditioning. There we sat like idiots, smiling and sweating.'

Naji hooted with laughter.

'You weren't interested in other girls for long, *ha*, Nabeel?' said Uncle. 'You see, Ruba, your mother was so beautiful your father fell in love with her almost in a second.'

I leant against Uncle Wadih on the sofa and the heat of him came through his clothes. I couldn't remember whether Papi was this warm or not because I couldn't remember ever having leant against him.

'Was she the most beautiful one?' I saw a pretty girl running and laughing, but the girl wasn't Mami.

'Yes,' said Uncle Wadih, as Mami came back in with a *rakweh* of coffee. 'But, then, all women are beautiful in one way or another. Your mother's a good woman – and a good wife, which is rarer. And at least there are still such women. Pearls among rubbish, *ya* Nabeel?'

Gazing at the shimmer of her silk shirt, I imagined Mami made of pearls: smooth polished face, smaller pearls for her eyes, and a row for her toes.

Over coffee Uncle said there was no hurry for him to be back at work, and he would stay awhile. Everyone looked pleased except for Mami, who stared into her tiny cup.

'What do you work as?' asked Naji, settling himself on the other side of Uncle.

'I work in a wood factory,' Uncle explained.

'What kind of things do you make?' asked Naji.

'Oh, all sorts of things. *Beauuuutiful* things.' Uncle's arms rose and fell so that his jacket crunched lightly.

'Do you make them?' Naji wanted to know.

'Stop bothering your uncle,' said Papi.

Naji glared at him. 'He doesn't think I'm a bother.' He looked up at Uncle. 'I've made things from wood – from sticks and things, just like you.'

Uncle laughed softly – a low drumbeat. It was a strange sound in our house, where grown-ups never laughed. 'No, I don't make them. The factory isn't in Beirut. Down in the city I deal with the business side.'

Business. The word reminded me of the dead man.

The following day Uncle Wadih went to visit the dead fat man.

'What? Even though he's dead?' Naji asked Teta.

'He's gone to see the man's family.' Sitting down on her bed, she handed me a hairbrush. 'Here, scratch my back with this, *habibti*. A thousand ants are dancing on it.' She lifted the back of her shirt to reveal it, broad, and pale, and I scratched.

'Now all over.' Teta's shoulders drooping and her head falling forwards.

When I finished, the brush went back on the table beside the blonde Virgin Mary with the bottle-top crown, but as Teta pulled down her shirt, her eyes were glistening.

'Did I brush too hard?' I peered at her. 'Did I, Teta?'

'No, my soul.' She took hold of my hand. 'You could never brush my back too hard.'

Leaning against the bedpost, Naji chewed his lip. 'Why are you crying? Did you know the dead man?'

'Yes.' She sighed and, taking a tissue out of her sleeve, dabbed her eyes. 'But I didn't like him.'

'Why are you crying, then?' asked Naji.

But Teta only sighed, pulled herself up and went out of the room.

As we crossed the road to go home, a heat-haze was rising from the engine of the parked cream Mercedes, and I heard the high-pitched laughter of little girls. Except it wasn't little girls.

The Rose Man's daughters were standing on the far side of the veranda with Uncle. Ghada, the younger one, had her hand over her mouth and laughter was escaping from beneath it. She was gazing at Uncle Wadih from under her eyelashes and holding her head at an angle that made it look as if it wasn't screwed onto her neck properly.

'What's she doing?' I asked, peering round the corner with Naji. But now Uncle leant down to say something in Samira's ear, and although she was the sensible sister, she unseamed into giggles too.

'What joke is he telling?' I started to go forwards, but Naji pulled me back.

'We mustn't. He wouldn't like it.'

Then Uncle started on something else. '"Se trouva fort dépourvue, quand la bise fut venue: pas un seul petit morceau de mouche ou de vermisseau." He was using a different voice, one he only used when he was talking to women. He had another for when he was talking to us.

Samira's arms were wrapped round herself, Ghada's fingers picked at the skirt of her blue dress, and both were gazing at Uncle as though he were Jesus.

Suddenly Uncle put up his hands the way people did when a gun was pointing at them. "Elle alla crier famine chez la fourmi sa voisine. La priant de lui prêter quelque grain pour subsister jusqu'à la saison nouvelle." He bent his head towards the sisters. 'That means the grasshopper was suffering with hunger.'

'Look!' giggled Naji. 'They're grown-up and they're still listening to the ant and the grasshopper!'

The two women were entranced. Samira clutched at her neck. 'That's beautiful. Did you hear how beautiful that was, Ghada? Did you hear the poetry?'

Ghada smiled the way unmarried girls smiled. 'Yes.'

'But that poem . . . The way you recited it was beautiful,' Samira declared.

Uncle gave a slight bow, and we went inside to wait for him. The weather was still sticky. Since yesterday it had felt as if the clouds must split like cloth and let out their load, yet still no drop fell from the dark sky.

Mami had gone out to buy food, but drinking cordial in the kitchen, we listened to the faint voices of Papi and the Rose Man in the next room.

'Maybe that's why Uncle's out on the veranda,' said Naji, suddenly angry. 'So he doesn't have to be in there.' He jerked his thumb towards the living room.

'What's wrong?'

Naji glared at the closed door. 'Him. He's always talking about the war. Uncle's not like that. He laughs and jokes and . . . knows how to be with people.'

We were finishing our second glass of cordial when Uncle Wadih came back inside. I clutched his jacket so he couldn't get away again. 'You were out there for ages.'

He looked surprised. 'They're lovely ladies.' It was the voice he used for me and Naji. 'Don't they deserve to have me talking to them?'

'How long are you going to stay?' I demanded.

Uncle glanced at the nearly empty glasses, then checked his jacket for fingermarks. There were none. 'I haven't been here a couple of days and you're thinking of me leaving already?'

'Will you stay till Christmas? Or are you going to marry Ghada and Samira and stay for ever?'

He laughed. 'Not for ever, my love. Not even till Chrismas.'

We followed him into the living room, where he told stories about life in Beirut. The sniping had got worse on the Green Line, he said. The young ones were bored and sat in shelled buildings looking out onto the other side and practising their shooting. He told the story of an old woman who had come out to buy bread; one of the soldiers took aim, then hesitated. His friend encouraged him but, with his finger on the trigger, the other couldn't shoot.

'Why not?' asked Naji.

'Because she reminded him of his grandmother.'

The Rose Man whistled softly. The taste of the cordial was sickly in my mouth, and I saw Teta picking her way through narrow streets between shelled buildings carrying a bag of bread. Did the old woman who wasn't shot make delicious sandwiches like Teta, or sling her carpets over the balcony railings and thump them with a beater of plaited willow till the dust jumped out?

'Now, if you're a Christian and die in West Beirut,' said the Rose Man, 'or a Muslim who dies in the East, they have to convert you before you can be buried. Imagine, you spend your whole life fighting for your religion, and the moment you die they convert you.'

'I don't like you living down there,' said Papi. 'Not any more.'

But Uncle brushed it off, settled back on the sofa and began another story. 'I had to cross Beirut for business the

44

other week. But let's make this clear, my friends, I wasn't going to go in my car. They'd have stopped me for sure, and if they had . . . well . . . I took a taxi.'

He leant back, resting his arms along the top of the sofa so that he looked like a lilac-winged bird. His black hair gleamed and the heavy-lidded eyes glanced between Papi and the Rose Man.

'But, you know, each one of those old brown Mercedes taxis is packed with a whole tribe: a man, his wife, the wife's cousin, the cousin's great-uncle, a nephew twice removed, his goat and the goat's fleas. The back bumpers are kissing the ground, the roof-rack's balancing a tower of luggage, and the boot has to be tied shut with a rope. These are the taxis of Beirut.'

He pinched my cheek and continued. On his way back, a checkpoint had sprung up where there had been none that morning, with Muslim militia guards checking cars. Everyone knew it was safer to travel by taxi – the guards know the taxi drivers and the taxi drivers know the militia – so Uncle's taxi was full, with two other men, a woman and her child.

He rubbed his hands round each other as if he were soaping them. 'So there we are, sitting targets, and nothing we can do. And the queue moves on by millimetres, the checkpoint draws nearer, and there's nothing to do but sit and smell the stink of humanity. When we draw up, the Kalashnikovs start waving in our faces and, of course, the soldier wants to see our cards.'

I waited to see what Uncle would do, how he would defeat them all. The Rose Man crossed and uncrossed his legs, and Naji cracked his knuckles. Only Papi, eyes fixed on Uncle, didn't move. His dull trousers and flecked grey jumper gave the impression of a boulder overgrown with moss. Fine tendrils and knotted vines of muscle climbed up his neck beneath the skin and vanished, twisting, beneath the too-long hair.

'What's on an identification card?' asked Naji.

'They take a man's life and reduce it to a couple of inches of paper,' scoffed Papi. 'It tells them not only that you're Christian or Muslim, but whether you're Maronite, Greek Catholic, Greek Orthodox, Sunni, Shi'a or Druze.'

'So this guard starts to check the cards, his rifle hanging into the car. He checks the man in front, but the woman's fumbling and taking her time – God knows where in that handbag she's got it – and the child's getting in her way, so the soldier moves on to the second man. After him there's only me and, I tell you, I'm squashed in there, my back stuck to the seat I'm so scared. I sit in the back of that car knowing that when he gets to me, maybe that'll be it. When he sees I'm a Maronite . . .'

Naji had cracked all his knuckles and they wouldn't crack again.

'The man beside me produces his card, and the guard nods. Now there's only me. And what am I to do? I'm fiddling about with my wallet to buy time, and just when I can't delay any longer, the woman finds her card and puts it into the guard's hands. Then he leans in with his eyes fixed on me. And I swear it's by the grace of Allah, by the grace of God Himself, that her child hears the gun tapping against the car. And, *ohhhh*, how he starts to cry – not just a mewling, but screaming at the top of his voice the way only a child can. That sound – unbearable! So the guard stood up, waved us on, and that was the end of the story.'

Everybody in the room softened and relaxed.

Soon the Rose Man left, and Papi fetched two bottles of beer. Thunder rumbled far off as he poured them. 'You didn't get it sorted out?' he asked Uncle Wadih.

'No. They tell me he might have lost everything: the whole business. I'll bet that was why his heart stopped beating.'

Papi took a gulp of beer. 'They buried him two days before you came.'

'Yes, I know.'

'We saw his funeral,' I piped up, but they weren't interested.

'And your shares?' Papi asked.

'Gone. That's what I get for trusting the man. Blight his life, he probably *ate* his way through my profits.'

'Never mind, my brother, never mind. You're still working and the money's still coming in.'

'You're right, that's business. You put money into a company and you may end up rich or you may never see it again. But work's bad in Beirut. No honest man has much money. Except the coffin-makers – they're the only ones who make an excellent living nowadays.'

Naji jumped onto the sofa beside Uncle. 'What did you do all morning?'

Uncle brightened as he put an arm round Naji's shoulder. 'You know what I did? I was near some woods where there were some big birds flying over – a hundred, maybe.'

I squeezed onto the sofa too. 'What kind?'

'Flamingos, they call them. They're big and bright pink – pink as your bum!' His face relaxed into an easy smile.

'Did you see them, Uncle?' I asked. 'Pink birds?'

'Of course I did! There were some fellows in the woods hunting and—'

'Not hunting the birds!' I'd seen men come out of the forest at the bottom of the hill sometimes with long gleaming rifles, strings of shiny bullets slung round their shoulders and limp bundles of small birds hanging from their belts, feathery brown bouquets that dangled as they walked.

'Of course hunting the flamingos,' Uncle replied, tugging my hair. 'What else? It's the migration season, and young men like that sort of thing.' He turned to Papi. 'Michel's boys. They were heading off as I left, so I went down with them for a while.'

He poured the rest of his beer. 'It's like the neck of a bottle,' he explained to Naji. 'There are narrow straits through the mountain ranges here, and the birds get channelled through them. There's no other way.'

'Did the men shoot any?' asked Naji, eagerly. 'Did they? Did they kill any?'

'They did.'

There was a distant crackle of lightning.

'Didn't you shoot too?' Naji wanted to know. 'You got some as well, didn't you?'

Uncle's body throbbed with laughter. 'It's been years since I went hunting, but they insisted so I had a go.'

Naji whooped, but I felt suddenly squashed tight between Uncle and the sofa arm.

By evening the thunder had passed. It hadn't rained and the clouds had cleared, leaving a clean sky dotted with the first stars. I wanted Mami to sit on my bed until I felt sleepy, and searched the house for her. But with the passing of the thunder she had vanished.

I stumbled, breathless, from room to room, but when I peered out through the net of the kitchen door, I found her. She was on the veranda, clutching the metal railings with both hands, while behind her Teta stood unmoving in the blackening twilight. They were staring across the road at the glowing white shape that was Uncle's Mercedes. It seemed to throb palely in the gloom, the grille on the front of the bonnet like bared teeth, the headlights large watching eyes.

I was about to push open the door and join them when I noticed the tears streaming down Mami's face. Deep sobs pumped her chest in and out, and the dip in her throat was quivering like a leaf.

Teta shifted uncomfortably from one foot to the other. 'What do you want with such things, my girl?' she asked, her voice thick with pity. 'Such things . . .'

As her chest shuddered, Mami's shirt fluttered in the dying light. Palm upwards, she stretched out a hand towards the dimly shining car.

'It's so *beautiful*,' she sobbed, swallowing in great gulps. 'I don't think . . . I don't think I ever saw anything so beautiful.'

Chapter Five

At first things seemed to be getting better with Uncle Wadih around. A few days after he'd arrived, Papi tucked in his shirt and, sitting at the table, slipped on his shoes. His hair was combed and shining wet, and when he looked up his face was kind. It was a good day, then.

Kneeling on a chair, I leant over the table. 'Are you going to open the shop today, Papi?'

'Yes. Don't we want to live?' Then, in a better tone, 'And don't you want to have books and go to school?'

I nodded. His face, although it had just been shaved, still looked sandstone rough. He gave my hair a friendly stroke as he passed into the kitchen, and a clatter came from behind the door as he picked up the ratchet to wind open the shop's metal shutters.

Mami ran her hand over his shoulder even though his sleeve was already smooth, and talked in a bright voice about nothing. 'I think there's coffee in the back from last time. Everything will be dusty, but it won't take long to wipe off. Maybe I'll come up later.'

Naji and I walked with him up the hill. Around us, the

morning heat unfolded, thin and quiet as a tendril of vine, and somewhere a cockerel crowed. I was surprised at how light the ratchet seemed to be today. When we got to the shop, Papi slotted it into the hole in the wall, and the metal crumpled as the shutters opened, their wavy sheets bending into a giant roll above the door.

Inside, the shop with its stone floor and high ceiling was cool. Silver gleamed on shelves that grew all the way up the back wall, and out of which pots and pans sprouted like fruit. To the left, knives glinted, their points hanging downwards, while beyond in the darkness was a mess of shapes: aprons, mops, buckets, glasses, water jugs, doormats, tea-towels and brightly coloured glass ornaments.

The lights flickered on, forcing the shadows to slither away, and as that other magic place vanished into the cracks and corners, the shop became the shop again.

Papi stood a moment looking, but we pattered in towards the counter and the shiny black till, our fingers ready to play over the large round numbers that stood up on metal sticks. Naji got there first, and something he pressed made the drawer fly open.

Papi stepped up. 'Don't play with that.'

'Why not?' Naji retorted.

I pushed it shut. There were only some coins, a few one- and five-lira notes inside.

It was a full half-hour before anyone came in. She was a fat woman with puffed-up orange hair and enormous clip earrings covered with chips of blue and green glass. A small shiny handbag hung from one arm. I counted three chins.

By the time I had taken her in, Papi was pulling a large pot off the bottom shelf. 'This one is good – well made.'

The rings on the fat fingers clicked against the metal as she took the pot in both hands, bouncing it gently up and down like a baby. But her head tilted back. 'No, not this one. It's too light. No, it's no good.' The three chins melted into one as she looked up. 'What about that one up there – the red one?'

Naji, who had been fussing with a pile of doormats, looked up.

Papi disappeared to the side of the shop and returned with a ladder. It clacked against the shelves and he started to climb the creaking mountain. He went slowly, never changing his pace or hesitating – so slowly that the painful creaking seemed to come not from the ladder but from him. When his head was bent so that it wouldn't bump the ceiling, he reached out and jigsawed the red pot out from among the others. A thick cloud of dust came off the top when he blew on it.

'Yes, I saw it on TV – I'm sure it was that one.'

With the pot balanced carefully in one hand, Papi inched his way down. First one foot then the other felt blindly for the next rung, free hand scraping on the flaking navy-blue ladder.

He was halfway down when the tutting came from below. 'No, no, it's wrong. It's not what I want, I can see from here. Don't bother bringing it down. Save yourself the trouble.'

Naji was glowering, his hands clenched in his pockets so they lifted his trousers and made his white socks show.

Papi said something about it not being a bother, and up he went again, the pot's lid clattering and shivering. His square face expressed nothing as he carried the ladder back to its place.

Now there was a soft tutting from among the knives, which clicked and flashed as the fat fingers examined them.

'Why doesn't she leave?' said Naji in an angry whisper. 'She's not going to buy anything. Why doesn't he tell her?'

She turned then and started walking towards the door. I watched the fleshy feet bulge over the tops of her heeled shoes at every step like soft, after-party balloons. But then they stopped and came back to the counter.

'Is this your newspaper? Are you selling it?' She fingered the pages lying open on the countertop. 'I passed the newsagent already, didn't I? Up that way?' Her arm rose and fell. 'And I forgot to buy one.'

'It's mine – but please . . .' As Papi closed it, folded it in half and offered it to her, the shiny bag unflapped, a shiny purse came out and a single lira was drawn from inside.

The breath was coming hard out of Naji's nostrils.

'No, no.' Papi held out a hand to stop her.

'Why not?' The brown note waved about as she spoke. 'It's your paper and I want to buy it. Times are not so easy now. Why be embarrassed?'

Beside me, Naji's face flushed to a deep red.

'No. Please.' Papi sank down a little into the counter. 'You should be ashamed of yourself. *Wallaow.*' He clicked his tongue.

She paused with the note still pinched between her fingers, then nodding, took the paper and left.

No one moved. We stared at Papi and he stared back at us. Out of the corner of my eye, I saw Naji's mouth working as if he wanted to speak, shout, or maybe cry, but he did none of those things.

Papi continued to stare at us, and his eyes were two deep wells of misery. Then Naji's heel scuffed the floor as he turned and left.

* * *

For the next quarter of an hour Papi paced, frowning and muttering to himself. Then he phoned Mami. 'I can't bear it any more,' he said, so she came up to tend the shop for the rest of the morning.

'My legs are hurting again,' I complained after Papi had left.

'It's only muscle cramps. You're growing up, that's all.'

I rubbed my calves. 'Then I don't want to. It's painful being stretched big. Besides, I'll have to be worried all the time like Teta, or sit all the time like Papi, or clean all the time like you, or be angry like Naji.'

Footsteps approached the door and Mami got to her feet with a tight customer-smile. But it wasn't a customer. Our doctor's daughter, Juhaina, had stopped off before when Mami was here, and she looked in now.

Yellow-veined hair and large sunglasses appeared, then the rest of her: a cigarette, a brown dress with a tight belt, gold-coloured shoes and handbag, and big gold jewellery.

'Sitting by yourself?' she said as she stepped past me, glinting like a fish and leaving a sting of perfume behind her.

'*Marhaba*, Juhaina.' Mami relaxed and looked pleased to see her friend.

Juhaina kissed the air near Mami's ears three times, her eyelids and lips shiny with makeup.

'You know my daughter.'

Juhaina turned to me with a smile and a voice crusted with sugar. 'Of course!' She took off her glasses. 'How are you, *chérie*? Are you helping your mother?' Pinching my cheek, she glanced disapprovingly at my dusty trousers, then took the chair Mami offered her. '*Phhht*,' she said, sitting down. 'Once you have children you're tied to the house. Don't you find that, Aida? Look at me. I only have one little

54

son, and even with a maid, I can hardly go out any more.'

I squatted behind the glass counter. Through the glass Mami looked small with big hair, while Juhaina's mouth was swollen: a thick red mouth with huge teeth. I took a can-opener off a hook, placed it on the edge of the counter and started turning the handle. Soon I would open the whole counter and beautiful things would pop out.

'I don't know how you manage to do so much, Aida. I can hardly cope just looking after the maid. She's supposed to do everything, but you need to follow her like a spy. You don't know when these people will steal something. You've got to be careful *tout le temps*.'

I had walked the can-opener all the way round the counter, but nothing wonderful had come out.

'Where does your maid come from? Sri Lanka?' I asked.

Juhaina looked at me as if I'd caught fire. 'No, she's a Filippina. They're better.' She turned back to Mami. 'She sends all her money to her family. She has a little baby, I think. In any case, once she gets started talking about her family, *je ne peux pas placer le mot*.'

'There are elephants in Sri Lanka. And crocodiles. My teacher Missizbel told us.'

Juhaina stared, the two streaks of colour on her cheeks standing out bright. 'Miss who?'

'She's their English teacher in school.'

'Ah, the one who gads about town in jeans and a ponytail with not a speck of makeup on to brighten that white face.' She tutted. 'A teacher should look respectable. A shop-girl has better taste than that.'

'I'm sure she's a good teacher. The children like her.'

'I saw her the other day, walking up to the next town by

herself – as if this is the country it was fifty years ago. What will people say?'

I rearranged some dusters according to their colour while Mami and Juhaina talked. Mami was chatting and laughing. She looked more alive somehow, and it struck me then that she seemed happier when she wasn't with Papi. Poor Papi. Nothing good ever happened to him. He finally felt well enough to open the shop, and customers like the fat woman came in to bother him. For Mami it was different: she met friends and had a good time.

Juhaina was showing Mami a little flat box.

'Look what I just bought. Snakeskin, the woman said.' She stroked the shiny purple scales. 'It's for face powder.'

'Is it really made out of a snake?' I asked, coming closer.

'*Bien sûr.* Here.' Juhaina handed it to Mami. 'What do you think?'

Mami fingered the gold clasp at the front. When she pressed it and the top bounced open, she looked at herself in the little mirror before closing it again. 'It's so pretty,' she said admiringly.

I managed to give it a stroke too, but it felt like oily little scabs. I didn't think it was pretty at all.

'Listen,' Juhaina said, taking back the box, 'I'm having some friends over for some drinks and a bite to eat. Why don't you come?'

'Oh, no, I can't.'

'Why not?'

'I . . . I'm too busy. Really.'

'It's only a small gathering, nothing fussy.'

Mami thanked her again but said she simply couldn't go.

'As you like, Aida,' said Juhaina, waving a hand, 'but as I say,

I don't know how you cope. The housework, two children and a husband . . .' She shook her head and the red lips pursed up tight. 'And now you have to take care of the shop as well.'

'It's only what most wives have to do.'

'Ha! Not these days. There's more to life than housekeeping, that's what I tell Fareed. It's a husband's duty to make sure his wife is happy, *n'est-ce pas*? "That's why I married you," I say to him. "So you would take care of me."'

'And what does he say?' asked Mami curiously.

'What is there for him to say but that he agrees?' She touched her stiff hair. 'No, *chérie*, a man should treat a woman like a woman.'

I left Mami in the shop. At home, I found Teta on the sofa and Naji chatting to Uncle Wadih.

'When are we going to the fair?' he asked. 'You said, remember?'

'Oh, soon. We'll go soon.'

Papi glanced up from the pile of papers he was sorting through in the dining room, serious papers with lists of numbers and his small writing on them. 'What's this?'

'Uncle Wadih's going to take us down to the Luna Park in Beirut,' said Naji.

'Down on the *autostrade*?'

Naji nodded. 'It's because I got such good marks in my test. I got —'

'You're going to a fair in West Beirut where they're killing each other like dogs?'

Naji's smile wilted.

'Nothing's happening around there,' said Uncle, from the sofa. 'Do you think' – he flattened his hands on his

57

chest – 'I'd take the children to a place where it's dangerous? People go into Beirut the whole time. I know where to go and where not to go.'

'My children aren't going anywhere.' Papi returned to his papers.

Teta wiped her mouth as though there was something bitter on her lips but said nothing. She looked miserable.

'We're going to Jbeil with school next week. How come we can go there?' I asked.

'That's a different place,' said Papi. 'You pass quickly through East Beirut to get to the coast road, that's all. There's no real danger.'

'He promised.' Naji turned to Uncle Wadih. 'You promised!'

'And I say no.' Papi started leafing through his papers again. He scribbled something, then rubbed his forehead.

Naji's face darkened. 'He promised. *He*'s not a coward. And you can't stop him taking us.'

Papi and Naji stared at one another.

'You can't stop him!' Naji exploded. 'You can't stop anyone doing anything! You can't even stop a stupid fat woman taking your newspaper!'

I waited for Papi to react, but nothing happened.

Naji swung round to Uncle. 'You'll still take us, won't you, Uncle? Won't you? You don't care what he says.'

Uncle gave a nose sigh. 'If your father says no, then we don't go, you understand? It's as your father wants.'

'But . . . you *promised*!'

'Naji . . .' Uncle shook his head.

Teta laid a hand on Naji's arm. 'Don't worry your father. Can't you see he's got his own troubles? Be good like your sister.'

My fingers made the new hole in my jumper bigger as I watched Naji stalk to the phone stool, take up a piece of paper he found there and begin to tear it into tiny bits. The more I felt sorry for Papi, the more Naji seemed to hate him.

Minutes passed without anyone saying a word, and suddenly I missed the sound of chopping, stirring and crockery that usually came from the kitchen; or the swish of the broom from outside; or the hiss of steam from the iron as it was set upright, the squeak of cloth against windows, the clatter of things being tidied away around the house.

Finally Uncle spoke: 'And you, my mother? Why are you so silent these days? Do you have more worries than you deserve as well?'

She snorted. 'What is my life but worries? Worries for these children, for you, for . . .' Her eyes squeezed shut a moment, vanishing into a hundred wrinkles. 'But why should life be anything else?'

Uncle gave a crooked smile. 'So, you've taken on the troubles of the world. You've started to see black in the sky.'

Slowly Teta's face folded in on itself, tears rising to her eyes like water on salted meat.

Papi pushed back his chair as if he meant to come over, but Uncle was quicker. 'What's this?' He put an arm round her shoulders. 'What, are you going to cry now and make my heart hurt?'

The tears fanned out over her face. 'And why shouldn't I cry? Why shouldn't I cry when Death is sniggering behind my shoulder?'

Naji's face twisted at the sight of Teta's tears.

'Have you been to the doctor without telling us?' Uncle leant close, suddenly concerned. 'Are you sick? Has he said anything?'

Papi watched anxiously.

'No doctor needs to tell me what's going to happen.'

'What are you talking about?'

A fresh tear grew big in the corner of one eye and plopped onto her breast. 'When bad dreams come almost every night now, do I need a clearer warning?'

'Dreams?' Uncle sat back, relieved. 'Dreams of what?'

'That the Virgin has forsaken me. That Death is close.'

The slightest smile played round Uncle's mouth, then flew away as he tightened his one-armed hug round her shoulders. 'What warning is that? Tell me, Mother.'

Teta's chest shook. 'That someone is going to die.'

Full of hate, Naji's eyes flicked to Papi and settled on him.

'I shall die soon, or if not me . . . God grant it's me and not one of you. And not the children . . . Not the children!' With the fingertips of her right hand together, she jabbed the centre of her chest, looking upwards. 'Allah, don't let it be anyone but me. Keep my children safe, and their children.' She rocked back and forth, stabbing her breastbone.

My leg had gone numb but I didn't dare move. I didn't dare do anything but watch them as they sat, Uncle's arm still clutched round her, rocking together. From the far side of the room, Papi watched too, his face taut and worried.

'Look.' Uncle spoke in a cheering voice. 'Here we all are, your two sons and your grandchildren' – he waved up the road – 'your daughter-in-law, all of us, and you can only cry.'

'What can you say to comfort me when the Virgin —'

'The Virgin?' Uncle's voice was sharper now. 'If the Virgin makes you cry, she's more trouble than she's worth. So the next time she appears bringing bad news, turn your back on her, give a good fart and dream of something else, that's what I advise.'

That evening while Mami cleaned the bathroom, I stood outside on the veranda watching the water rush out of the pipe in the wall. Some twigs lay across the drain, forcing it to flow out of the concrete channel, worm its way across the tiles and trickle down into the road. It carried clumps of powder and yellow, fizzing suds – yellow as the flames on the cover of Uncle's book.

Beside the wall, the cactus drooped a little lower than before. One of its arms had shrivelled from lack of water. Just as I thought of watering it myself, the kitchen door opened and Uncle stepped out to smoke a cigarette. He came and stood beside me, leaning on top of the railings.

'And what are you doing all alone out here?'

'Nothing.'

He struck a match that threw a glow onto his cheeks and nose, and I noticed with a little shock how long and slender his thumb was, more like a finger than a thumb.

'So you're still angry with me for shooting flamingos, *ha*?'

I didn't reply, just watched the smoke drift slowly upwards.

'There are worse things you can do to a bird, you know.'

'Worse than shooting it?'

'I'll tell you a story. Teta says you like stories.'

'Is Teta all right now?'

He nodded. 'She's all right.'

'What was the matter with her?'

'She's got something into her head that she won't let go of, even though it makes her sad.' He took a puff and breathed the smoke out of his nostrils. 'Sometimes, my love, we can't see the good for the bad. "Which one of us listens to the hymn of the brook when the tempest speaks?"'

'What brook?' I asked, staring at the hissing stream oozing across the tiles, but Uncle only smiled and blew out more smoke into the evening air. 'Tell me the story.'

'Ah, yes, the story. Well, as it is in most stories, a young man falls in love with a beautiful woman. Of course he wants to make her love him too, so he does everything he can think of. He buys her expensive gifts, gives parties for her, all sorts of things.'

'Uncle,' I interrupted, 'do all women love expensive pretty things?'

He nodded. 'Most of them, yes.'

'Is that why he gives her those presents? To keep her close and stop her running away?' I thought of Mami, and fear slid in through the spaces between my ribs.

'Yes. But with this woman, nothing works. She doesn't love the man and marries someone else. But he's spent so much money trying to get her that eventually he has nothing left except a pet bird, a falcon.' A bent finger of ash fell off the end of Uncle's cigarette into the yellow stream. 'So he goes with this bird of his to live on a farm in the country.'

'Where? Up in the mountains where the cedars are?'

Uncle smiled. 'It doesn't matter where. The man goes out into the countryside. He's lost all he has, but he isn't miserable. He doesn't whine about it, just goes and lives a simple life in the country. He has no luxuries, none of the things he's been used to, and his pet falcon becomes the most important thing in his life. Well, one day the beautiful woman's husband dies.'

'Was her husband richer than the first man? Is that why she married him?'

'Perhaps. He certainly was very rich. Anyway, he dies and leaves her with a son. Now that they're alone, the woman and her son go into the country for a holiday, and there the little boy meets the man and plays with the falcon. Everything goes well until the little boy falls sick. He grows so sick that his mother is worried. She wants to make him better and asks him what he wants. And what do you think he says?'

I shrugged. 'Fried potatoes?'

'Why would he want fried potatoes?' Uncle laughed. 'No, it's the falcon he wants, the man's falcon, the one thing he has in all the world. So the mother goes to ask for it. Of course, when the man sees her carriage coming down the road, he's amazed. What has he got to offer this beautiful woman now? He's poor and has nothing. He doesn't even have any food to give her. So he kills his falcon and cooks it.'

'No!'

'He cooks his pet, which he loves so much, and together they eat it. And when they finish, she tells him why she has come, but there is no bird to give the boy any longer.'

'Does the boy die?' A fresh gush of yellow water poured across the veranda, past the cactus and down the step into the gutter.

'Yes, he dies. Now isn't that more terrible than shooting a bird?' He stubbed out his cigarette on the railing, dropped it and straightened up.

'Look at the yellow. Mami says not to touch it.'

Uncle glanced down. 'That's right. You be careful, it might make you sick.'

'Why would it make me sick?'

'Because it's poisonous.'

I stepped back. The tiniest splash would turn me into something dead. 'Poison?' I felt different suddenly: ill because the poison stream might already have got me, and unhappy because it was Uncle who had brought fear out onto the veranda with him. Everything had gone right at first, but now it was all going wrong. If Mami wanted to be rich and was happier away from Papi, she might leave us and I'd never be able to find her again. Teta might die just like she said, and then there would only be me, and Naji and Papi who didn't get on any more.

I touched the brown hand that hung lazily over the railings and pushed the question out of my mouth. 'Uncle, what happened to Papi that day he changed? When I was little. When you were here.'

Uncle blinked as though I'd woken him up. He opened his mouth to say something, then shut it again. 'You don't know, *ha*?' He stood up. 'No, why should you?'

It was then that the idea came to me. Perhaps I could help Papi. If the witch had put a curse on him, maybe the evil eye in my pocket could undo it.

Chapter Six

A week later on a schoolday evening, Karim and I walked in silence down the main street, past trees that were hushed and motionless as if they too were scared. Beneath one, a couple of ancient men sat on tiny stools sipping coffee, and their small eyes, embedded in wrinkles, followed us as we passed.

I counted the shop signs that stuck out sideways into the street, followed the lines of washing that hung on the terraces above them, but that didn't help. The laundryman stepped out of his shop in a white vest, his neck and hairy chest gleaming wet. He stood for a moment in the cloud of steam, then turned back inside, and I thought of how his cousin's husband was supposed to be a spy for the *mukhabarat*.

By the time we'd walked up another slope and reached the high road the silence had thickened. Below us on the left the valley was green and still, while on the far side the Sannine mountains, which had been cut out jagged by someone and glued onto the blue sky, were already covered with snow. The buildings grew further apart, and before long only the odd house fronted the road. White stone walls and pale orange roofs peered from between the trees then vanished again.

Finally we were there. White stones lay in piles where the wall round the witch's yard had fallen down so that now only a few rocks set in a line marked the plot – a few rocks that couldn't stop us getting in.

'Are you afraid?' I asked Karim.

'No.' He didn't sound sure. 'And you *have* to come,' he added, as if he'd guessed my thoughts.

'I was going to! It was me who asked you to come, wasn't it? I'm the one who has to speak to her.'

It was autumn, and the light near the horizon was dying fast. Small clouds stretched in strips above the valley, and there was a smell of burning pine needles from a bonfire someone must have lit down the hill. I knew that in the forest the ground was covered with dry pine needles now, and I wished I was there. Purple crocuses had sprouted in the last couple of days, and furry whiskered grasses stood tall on strong, thin stems.

I glanced back. The street was silent. No car or person came from either direction to help us. I turned back, and the sky was blocked out by the witch's house with its three night-filled trees. Glowing dully, the broken fountain stood in the middle of a few paving-stones, with nothing in it except an empty plastic bottle. It reminded me of the Roman ruins in the next village where we sometimes went to play among the fallen columns and mosaics. There weren't many houses as old or grand as this one.

'No one's home,' said Karim. There were no lights on in the house: the high arched windows were dark.

'Come on.' I stepped over the broken wall. 'Where else would she be?'

Small stones scraped against the soles of my shoes, and Karim hurried after me.

I stopped. 'Is that you whimpering?'

'No.' He squirmed and tugged at his collar.

'Well, don't stand so close.' I waggled my shoulder to create some space between us. 'I can't move if you're up against me.'

The fingers and joints of the tallest tree flexed themselves overhead, creaking in the breeze. Then my heart jumped so high I almost spat it out, and at the same time Karim jolted. His fingers closed round my arm. 'Did you hear it?'

The sound came again: a low cackle, then a complaining *chuck-chuck-chuck.*

'It's all right,' I sighed. 'It's chickens. In the shed.' I pointed to the shack in the corner of the yard made of old planks nailed roughly together.

A car's headlights went by in a flash, then faded. The big tree over the fence groaned again, and when I glanced up, I saw an open-mouthed, astonished-looking moon balanced on the roof of the old house. 'Come on,' I said again, but my voice sounded small.

Karim shook the back of my coat. 'But she eats cats,' he blurted.

'I – I know.' I grasped the glass eye in my pocket for protection, but couldn't help thinking of Teta's bad dreams that someone was going to die, and that that someone could be me.

'Karim!' A light had come on deep inside the house, thick and webbed as a glow at the bottom of a black pond.

When Karim saw it, his face turned soft. 'What are you doing?' he hissed.

'I'm going to talk to her. Why else did I come?' I would show her the evil eye, and tell her straight out to lift the curse off Papi.

Every nerve was singing, and a few steps behind, Karim shuffled, ready to shoot out of that place as fast as the flick of a finger.

The shutters were open against the wall, but there were still no lights on in the outer rooms.

'You're going to look *inside*?' gasped Karim.

'She lives inside, doesn't she?'

'Why don't you just knock on the door?'

I didn't answer.

He padded after me round the house. 'But I'm not going to look in at the windows.'

A lump rose in my throat. I swallowed it down, stood on tiptoe and, with my fingers on the cool stone ledge, looked into the first room. It was a kitchen.

'There's nothing,' I reported. 'A sink, a bucket, a white-tiled floor.' It was strangely normal.

Faster now, I slipped quickly past the front door to where there was another, larger window. Not a sound came from inside.

'But she might really *be* in there,' warned Karim as I placed my fingers on the second ledge.

'I know. Stop nagging. I'll knock on the door in a minute and then we'll leave.'

I wondered if Ali's story about the witch being friends with the devil was true, and whether she ever invited him inside for a meal. Would the devil sit down to a dish of green beans or okra, or did he only eat red meat?

Karim's mouth was suddenly at my ear. 'Is she there?' But I pushed past him to the corner of the house, leaving him beneath the window, arms curled into his chest.

It was darker round the corner, dark as wine, but there was nothing. 'Only the veranda at the end,' I whispered as I came back.

The curious moon had floated further up to watch us. And then Karim gave a long gasp as if he'd just come up from the bottom of a swimming-pool. He was peering in at the window, his body rigid, his eyes almost popping out of his head.

'What?' I stopped where I was. 'What is it?'

Karim had grown roots. For a second I thought he might remain there, an ornament beside the house for the rest of time. The witch would jump out now. Or now. Or now. We would be fried up for her dinner. Or she might turn me into a chicken, and then Mami would buy me from the market and hum softly as she plucked and smeared me with garlic.

But then the ornament turned and ran, scattering pebbles behind it.

'Wait! Wait! You can't leave! I've still got to speak to her!'

But Karim didn't stop. He didn't cry out or slow down. For a moment I was undecided, but at the sight of his scrawny backside disappearing into the gloom, my muscles sparked alive and I raced after him.

When I reached the chicken shed, though, I had an idea. I stopped just long enough to lift the latch and let the door swing open. Her chickens would wander out and she'd spend hours rounding them up. It would serve her right for everything she'd done.

I jumped over the remains of the wall and ran on, never once looking at what might be galloping close behind me, hungrily licking its lips, reaching clawed fingers towards my throat and heart.

Back in front of Karim's building and panting like a dog in July, I held his cold hands and looked back now to make sure nothing was creeping up to us through the shadows. Light shone comfortingly from a bulb above the main door, yet Karim was staring through me, his lips parted like a fish's.

'What did you see?' I asked again.

He yanked away his hands and sat down heavily on the steps. It wasn't until four cars had gone by, croaking and straining up the hill, that he spoke.

'Her.' His eyes grew large. 'I saw *her*.'

'Is that all?' I leant closer. 'Did she see you?'

His teeth scraped over his bottom lip. 'There was a noise and I looked up and she was there. Except it wasn't—' He swallowed hard. 'I thought it was the witch, but . . .' his voice came out so low I could barely hear it '. . . it was a ghost.'

I sat down, relieved. 'Who believes in ghosts?' I tried to laugh, but the hairs at my temples were tingling. 'So what does a ghost look like?'

He glared at me accusingly. 'Like her, only . . . more scary. There was fog, white fog, all round her face!'

'What did she do when she saw you?'

'Nothing. She saw me, that's all, and that was enough.' He rubbed his nose hard with the heel of his hand. 'But there was someone else too. Something else.'

The weave of Karim's coat stood out sharply in plaited rows of blue and grey. A light flickered from a balcony above. 'Amal.'

I got to my feet. 'What are you talking about? Have your brains turned to slop?'

'She was there! I looked past the witch – I mean the ghost – and Amal was behind her.' He looked up at me defiantly. 'It was her!'

Chapter Seven

The next day she was sitting at the front of the bus taking us on our school trip to Jbeil. She didn't look up as I hurried by. Everyone else filed straight past too. Nobody sat next to her. When Karim saw her, he hopped off the bus again and got on through the back doors instead. Sliding onto the seat beside me, he gripped the metal bar in front of him with both hands, eyes fixed on Amal. But she didn't turn round.

As we set off, I watched her fiddle with her hair. Didn't she mind not having any friends?

'Maybe she saw us yesterday,' whispered Karim.

But even if she had, she didn't seem interested now.

'What was she doing in the witch's house?' I asked, but Karim didn't know. The mystery round Amal had thickened like beaten egg whites. Who was she? What sort of life did she have?

I thought about her all the way out of Ein Douwra. The road wound down and down round hairpin bends that made the tyres squeak. Karim and I swayed from side to side, our fingers clinging to the seats. The bus went into several large pits in the road, falling and rising again. Bags slipped to the floor; Karim's apple rolled to the back, then thudded and zigzagged its way forwards again.

We passed shrines and clothes shops, a thin dog chewing a stick, and a man selling clay pots on the dusty verge. Beirut, which lay below us in pale building blocks beside the sea, grew closer. We'd have to pass through part of it and get to the other side to reach Jbeil, and it was going to be wonderful: all the pictures in our history and geography books showed a beautiful Beirut with palm trees and orange-roofed buildings and a glittering blue sea; groves of pine trees, clean roads, buses and old-fashioned cars, large squares, fruit markets and gleaming rows of boats tied up in the harbour.

But there was no bright clean city beside the sea. There was only greyness, a place worse than Ein Douwra. The tall buildings were drab and old. Most needed to be repaired. One looked as though it was made of sand and had been half blown away by a strong wind. It was leaning and bent with black gaps for windows, the corners of two balconies missing and holes where the walls on the right-hand side had fallen away. On both sides of the road hung signs and tattered advertisements in Arabic, French and English.

I turned round to the seat behind. 'Naji, when will we get to Beirut?'

He yawned. 'This is it.'

There was hooting and shouting. A mess of cars jammed the narrow street ahead. One had a big dent in its side and a smashed wing-mirror. Black smoke spewed out of another, its driver leaning out of the window waving his arm and hooting his horn.

The next road was no better. As we passed, I saw an alley piled high with rubbish: plastic bottles, an empty oil barrel, a sofa, an exhaust pipe, a doll. A few minutes later we drove past a boy sitting on the pavement watching cars. The huge block of flats behind him had been burrowed into by giant mice that had left a million holes and hollowed out the centre, until the building was nothing but a thin crust of shell with rain-stained walls. On one balcony, strings of faded washing hung out to dry.

The other children on the bus chattered and laughed. Amal was breathing rounds of mist onto the window and drawing faces in them. Naji and Karim were telling each other jokes. No one seemed to care that this wasn't the beautiful city beside the sea from our schoolbooks. Perhaps all beautiful things crumbled this way in the end. Perhaps something happened that made them change, like flowers or like the seasons or like Papi.

Suddenly we were out of the buildings and on a wide straight road that followed the coast. Cars moved faster here, speeding and shifting from lane to lane, and to our left, the sea was a dull grey-blue, blocked out by apartment buildings at one moment and in view the next. On the banks beside the road and along the shoreline, more rubbish lay scattered like some ugly new weed.

The waves caught the light and flicked it back into my eyes. We passed shops selling clothes, others selling pastries and sweets, but mostly there were just tall grey buildings speckled with bullet-holes, long metal poles sticking out of their walls like broken bones.

The first school bus had already emptied out its load of children when we arrived in Jbeil. Mrs Atallah was waiting:

she took a last drag at her cigarette and ground it underfoot. 'There are two other teachers,' she announced wearily. 'You'll stay with one of us so that you learn something.'

We walked, ran, skipped and hopped across the small bridge to the castle, Mrs Atallah's voice fading behind us. With its dry brown walls and row of arches, it was smaller than I had expected. The earth was sandy, with bushes and rocks but few trees, while beyond lay the sea and a curved beach that ended in an outcrop of rocks.

Karim wanted to go inside and headed off by himself, but Naji and I walked around on the sand. We found dry stone walls in the ground and followed them for a while. Below us, the sea carried a tiny boat across the horizon, and a little way to our left Mr James in his straw hat was adjusting his glasses and speaking aloud to himself as the boys in his group chased each other.

'This was where Byblos was originally located – just the space here on the clifftop. It's the oldest city, they say. First came the Canaanites, then the Phoenicians, the Persians, then the Romans, the Byzantines, the Arabs, the Crusaders and the Ottomans.' He took a step back as a boy dived past him. 'This is where Alexander the Great was welcomed, where the Egyptians traded to get cedar resin to make their mummies, where the alphabet was invented, and where glass and purple dye were first made.'

I lost my balance and jumped off a stone. 'Mrs Atallah taught us about the purple!' I told Naji. 'They got it from sea snails!' It was the only history lesson I remembered. 'But what's Byblos?'

'It's just another name for Jbeil.'

'How come it has two names?'

Naji gave a great sigh and rolled his eyes at my ignorance. 'Because it's the Roman name.' He looked down at me from the heights of the fifth year. 'That's why they call the Bible the Bible: because of Byblos.'

Mr James took off his straw hat and rubbed his pale hair. 'And over there,' he continued, squinting towards the edge of the cliff, 'is where they found the skeletons.'

There was one final shout and the boys stopped running.

'Like when you dead?' asked one, struggling to put the English words together. He pointed to a red-roofed house on the cliff edge. 'In the red house?'

'No, no, not there.' Mr James sounded annoyed. 'That's an Ottoman house. No – the huts were underneath. If you hadn't been running around . . . Well, that's how they buried them: in jars, curled up like this.' He crouched on his heels and pushed his chin into his chest.

I skipped off to find Naji among some columns. 'Mr James says there are dead people in jars over there.'

'Go away, I'm searching for things.'

'What things?'

He shrugged. 'Just things.'

After we'd found them, Mr James came and told us what our things were: parts of an old railway track, a Phoenician anchor in some thorny bushes, bits of Egyptian statues and two Roman signs. Closer to the sea, he said, there had been royal tombs once, which seemed a strange place to choose, near all the rubbish that had been thrown on the beach. 'And there's writing next to the king's tomb,' he said.

'What does it say?' Naji asked.

'It says . . .' Mr James spoke slowly, his voice suddenly low to scare us '. . . it says, "Take care, for death is below you."'

Another group appeared and we were sent to the castle. My feet slid about in the stony dirt as I ran after Naji. It wasn't far to the entrance, but when we got there two bullies were teasing Karim, pulling his hair and blocking his way.

'You can't get past – we're Crusaders, and you're a Muslim barbarian. We're not letting you in.'

His friend made a gun out of his thumb and finger. 'Let's shoot the invader! *Pack! Pack!* I got him in the shoulder! *Puh-puh-puh-puh-puh-puh-puh!*' The gun had turned into a machine-gun.

Karim was pushed over. 'Don't you know that's why the Christians built this castle? To keep you out?'

I didn't understand. 'What are they talking about?' I asked Naji, but just then Mrs Atallah's head appeared in a window.

'What are you children doing? Stop getting yourselves dirty! What will your parents say? Karim, get up.' She tutted. 'Where have we got to when boys your age are scratching in the dirt like chickens?'

Karim got up and vanished inside the castle, but Naji and I wandered into the narrow cobbled streets of the town which threaded and criss-crossed each other.

'Leave me alone,' said Naji. 'Why are you always following me?' But I didn't want to leave him alone and, anyway, I couldn't have found my way back now.

He stopped in front of a tiny shop and, squatting down, stared for a long time at some snail and fish fossils in the window. Then he emptied his pockets and counted his money.

'But Naji, are you really going to spend all your money on an old fish?' I called after him as he went in.

Awnings stretched overhead, shading the twisting street. Outside on the pavements, shirts and coats hung from poles in colourful bunches, baskets of shoes and boxes of books stood crammed side by side, and men sat drinking coffee at small tables set out in patches of morning sun.

Then my eye snagged on something. A familiar shape. The light and shade on the street shivered as a gust made the awnings flutter. And the familiar shape drinking coffee halfway down the street wavered. A second man at the table wearing sunglasses gestured with his hands. He took a piece of paper from the breast pocket of his jacket, set it on the table and nodded. Another gust, and the street shimmered again.

'Uncle?'

Nothing. I tried louder.

'Uncle Wadih?'

The man I thought was Uncle turned round. For a moment he didn't move. Then he quickly stood up and, with a couple of strides, vanished into the coffee shop.

I ran down the road. The man in the sunglasses looked surprised. He folded the piece of paper and put it back into his pocket. 'Where's Uncle?' I asked him, but he only gulped down the rest of his coffee. I looked inside but Uncle must have gone into the back of the shop because I couldn't see him.

'Hey!' Naji had bought what he wanted. 'Are you coming or not?'

I took one more look inside the coffee shop before joining him. 'It was Uncle. I saw him over there with that man.'

Naji stopped and glanced back. 'Don't be stupid.' He opened his little brown paper bag, took out a fish shape in a stone and turned it in his hand.

I tried to tell him again but he wouldn't believe me.

'Didn't you see Uncle in Ein Douwra?' He waved the dead fish in front of my face. 'Weren't you there when he dropped us off?'

Perhaps Naji was right. I wasn't sure any more.

On the way back, my thoughts flitted between Amal and Uncle as I stared out of the window. Down in a gully, a black car lay crushed. Further along, another was parked, its roof and bonnet weighed down with crates of fruit and vegetables. A group of young men lay stretched out on an island of weeds and rubbish in the middle of a busy round-about, eating oranges.

But when we got back to the schoolyard it was Mami who was waiting for us.

'Where's Uncle?' asked Naji.

The old brown car clanked and whirred as it moved off. 'He's gone. He left this morning.'

'Where to?' I asked. 'Did he go to Jbeil?'

Mami gave me a surprised look. 'What would he want to go there for? He got a phone call, and decided it was time to go home.'

And when we got back, it was true. Uncle had vanished into nothing, almost as if he had never been there at all.

Chapter Eight

Perhaps it was because Uncle wasn't there, or because I hadn't spoken to the witch and made her lift her curse, but after Jbeil things changed. I put away the glass eye in my drawer. On the veranda, the jasmines and fuchsias shrivelled. The geraniums scattered blackened petals round the cans that had once contained cooking grease and milk powder, and still showed happy cows and brilliant-toothed children. Indoors, Mami and Teta grew quieter and sadder, and Papi went back to how he'd been before.

'Is that why you look at that photo so much?' I asked Mami. 'Because you miss Uncle?'

She was measuring out almonds and dried fruit, but turned away quickly to search in a cupboard. It was the evening of Eid el Burbara, and our kitchen was warm with the smell of wheat, fennel, anise and cinnamon coming from the pot Teta was stirring.

'We – we're out of nuts,' said Mami. 'I'll go and buy some more.' She wiped her hands, fetched her purse and left, her face flushed with heat.

Bubbles popped and clucked in the pot. Teta had stopped stirring. 'What photo?'

'The one you gave me.' We'd been looking through old pictures, and Teta had handed me one of a young woman with long black hair. There were pine trees and ruins around her, large blocks of stone and a temple. She was jumping off one of the blocks to the ground, flying through the air with her arms and legs stretched out in a star shape. Her hair was fanned out, her mouth open in a scream-laugh, and watching from one side were Papi and Uncle, looking much younger. I didn't realize the girl was Mami until Teta told me. 'Whenever she looks at it, she gets sad.'

Teta frowned into the pot and started stirring the *burbara* again. I stole two almonds and a dried apricot, but she didn't notice.

'Teta, tell me a story.'

She blinked as though I'd woken her. 'What?'

'A story.'

'Not now, *habibti*.'

'Please. Tell me the one about the boy who wants the moon.' Even if she didn't feel like it, she might tell her favourite story, the one she told most often.

Teta spoke slowly, as if she was making up the story for the first time. 'She would look up at the moon, this girl, and my God, how beautiful it was.'

'Girl? I thought it was a boy. It's always a boy.'

Teta tipped her head back to say no. 'Tonight it's a girl. And the moon was so beautiful she couldn't stop looking at it. Night after night, all she could do was sit and look, always up, up at the moon.

'Well, so she went to her mother and she said, "I want the moon."'

There was a long silence. 'Aren't you going to finish it?'

Teta nodded. 'The mother said, "You want the moon?" But she couldn't do anything to help her child. So what could the girl do? She tried jumping but that didn't work. She reached up as high as she could but that didn't work either. So she got a ladder, the longest ladder she could find, and she started to climb.'

I saw a girl hauling herself slowly up the ladder in Papi's shop, past the pots and pans, past the roof and up into the sky.

'There were hundreds of stars, thousands of them, but they weren't good enough – no, not good enough for this girl. This girl wanted the moon.'

I crunched another almond.

'She carried on climbing and climbing, never stopping to rest, never stopping at all, getting further and further away. But then she began to miss her family.'

'You mean her mother,' I said.

'Yes, yes, her mother.'

'What did the girl do?' I'd heard this story dozens of times, but still hoped it would end differently.

'Do?' Teta looked up. 'She missed her home, that's all.'

Teta never told what happened – whether the boy who had turned into a girl tonight ever reached the moon. It always ended this way.

'What is it, Teta?' Tears were creeping down her face.

'Nothing, *habibti*, nothing. It's just the steam.' She reached into her top, pulled out a tissue and pressed it to each eye. But the tears continued to come.

'Teta, don't cry. Shall I stir? I'll get Papi.' But I thought again. On Eid el Burbara, Papi was always especially moody and tense because he didn't like masks. 'Or shall I go out and find Mami?'

'No, my love, no, your mother doesn't need any more bothering.' But then the tears welled up again. 'It makes me think of my own poor mother. When it was cold she'd rub my hands inside hers – inside her hard, hard hands – until they got warm.' She licked the tears from her lips. 'You've seen her picture. Didn't you notice how kind her eyes were? She could see into heaven with those eyes. She stroked my sister's head when she was sick – for hours she would sit there without stopping because it soothed the girl, and she asked my father how it could be that she knew how to cure a sick goat but not her own sick child. She loved each of her children as if we were her living heart, just the way I love all of you.' Her mouth quivered and she crossed herself, the spoon still in her hand. '*Ach*, *ya* Allah, what have I done for things to be this way?'

But it wasn't Teta's fault, and it made me feel sick to see her cry.

'Do you still think someone's going to die?' I asked.

'Die? Who can stop thinking of the dead – the fortunate dead, God rest their souls? Your grandfather, who decided to drop to the earth one day and leave me here. Where did he go without me since the day we married? Nowhere. So why did he take it into his head that day? I swear he did it on purpose, and I have the heart of a mountain herder that won't stop beating till I'm a hundred and twenty. He'd had enough of worries so he left me here with them all, and no one to take care of the family except for this old woman.

But what am I to do in the face of such problems?' She looked into the pot as if it might hold the answer.

Teta had stopped crying and I was helping her dice apricots when Naji walked in with a growl. He was wearing his mask, a brown bear-face with a large mouth. 'Did you bring mine?' I asked.

It was in the bag he handed me, a green-skinned monster with a bulb nose, black teeth and candy-floss hair. I caressed it lovingly.

Teta's mood had tightened. 'Don't you dare go near your father in those things,' she warned in her you'd-better-not voice.

'Why not? Is he scared of them?' Naji poked a finger through the eyehole of his mask, bending the plastic shell so the bear grinned.

'Are we going to have the same problem every year? You know to keep them away from him. Wear them outside, only don't let him see them.'

'But why?' he persisted.

'Don't carry the ladder sideways, *ya* Naji.'

'Fine, who cares?' Naji shrugged and walked out of the front door.

'Always doing things the difficult way,' muttered Teta.

'Teta, why can't Karim do Burbara with us? I was going to help him choose a mask and everything. He would have looked wonderful in a lizard one!' I watched Teta drop the fruit into the pot.

'They're Muslims.'

'So what?'

'Listen to the child! She wants Muslims to celebrate the festival of a Christian martyr.' She shook her head at my stupidity. I hadn't liked the story the teacher had told us about Saint Burbara: how she was kept in the tower by her father and how he chopped off her head when she said she was a Christian. I didn't see why he should have got so angry about it – unless she'd stopped cooking his meals too, and in that case she should have carried on cooking and kept quiet about being a Christian. That way she'd have lived longer.

'Mustn't Karim eat the sweets or the *burbara*?'

'That boy needs to eat. He's as skinny as a length of string.'

'He can come over afterwards, then?'

'Of course.' She dropped the fruit into the pot with some more spices.

'But Teta, what does it mean, being a Muslim? Is it bad?'

'Is Karim bad?'

'No.'

'Well then.'

I thought back to Jbeil. 'Does it make him different from us?'

'Before the war we all lived together in the same villages, no matter what our religion. Now we live mostly in different villages and in different regions. There are still a few Muslims here, but not many. They don't dress any differently from us and they're part of the village the same as we are.'

Outside, in the cold December night, Naji was pulling up weeds from the side of the road. He didn't want to go round the houses with me, but I begged till he gave in. We went to the Rose Man's first.

'Be happy you have the intestines to eat such things,' mumbled Samira as she offered us nougat. 'What with this war, I can't stomach a thing.'

When we'd done the block of flats opposite we knocked

on Karim's door and brought him home with us, passing other masked children along the road. As we neared home, we saw Juhaina waiting in her car with the motor running while her maid handed a tray of cakes to Mami.

Juhaina hooted. '*Yalla, ça suffit*,' came her voice. 'Do you want me to be attacked by all these children while you hide in my friend's kitchen?'

Mami went to church afterwards, and Teta dished out the *burbara* for us, muttering, 'What's that woman thinking, giving us her left-over cake? The country's bursting with the poor and the hungry; is it us who need her charity? And not even the decency to come in herself.'

Then she stood back, enjoying the way Karim shovelled the *burbara* into his mouth. She was even more pleased when he took a second helping.

Naji had been snappish all evening, but now he pushed back his chair. 'Let's go and play. Come on.'

The door to the living room where Papi was sitting was closed.

'What are we going to play?' asked Karim.

Naji pulled on his mask. ' Chase.' He had turned all friendly now. 'The bear will have to chase because he's the fastest, and whoever he catches first is the loser.' He took off the mask and looked from me to Karim. 'Who wants to be the bear?'

'But you wouldn't let me try it on earlier,' I reminded him. 'Why are you letting us wear it now?'

Karim didn't care. 'I haven't worn a mask yet, so it should be me.'

'But Naji, we're not supposed to wear them inside. If Papi sees—'

'We won't go in there,' said Naji.

Karim looked funny with a bear-face. 'Get ready. One, two –' he started running '– three!'

With a yell, I sped down the hall, into the dining room – twice round the table, back to the hall and into the bathroom – the door nearly closed, opened again as Karim pushed against it, then shut. There was a moment's silence, then I heard him move away.

When I opened the door there was no one outside, only a flash of Karim's green jumper as he vanished through the living-room door.

'Karim! No!'

When I got there, a thin bear was hanging onto Naji's sleeve singing, 'I win! I win!'

The world stopped, except for Karim's song. Papi seemed to shake as he rose, the mark on his forehead dark against his bleached face. Worry beads were strewn across the floor, their string snapped.

'I won! It only took me a minute and I won! I saw you run in here!'

Naji watched calmly as Papi stood rocking and trembling, his black eyes filled with a deeper blackness. There might have been a crack like stone breaking, then Papi was flowing across the room. Nothing else moved – the walls, the plastic flowers, the tray of cigarettes, an orange colouring pencil sticking out from under the sofa. They were stiller than real life, still as only photographs can be.

Papi moved towards the plastic-headed bear. He grew tall as the ceiling and Karim's head fell back as he looked up at him. Naji remained frozen as, with mad eyes, Papi jerked the bear back by the shoulder and roughly took off Karim's mask.

It lay a long time in Papi's hands, staring up at him.

Karim looked terrified. When Papi moved, Karim's arm came up protectively. But Papi didn't hit him. Instead, holding the mask in one hand and gritting his teeth, he stuck two fingers right into the eyeholes, forced them in until they were halfway through and wouldn't go any further.

Karim's arm fell as the two fingers twisted left then right, left then right, as if Papi wanted to get them further in; as if he wanted to mash the bear's eyes right up. I knew then that he was crazy.

A rope of vein stretched up the side of his neck to the rock jaw, and above it, his face was clenched. Naji gasped. The fingers ground left and right in the eyeholes, and a thread of blood zigzagged down the white inside of the bear-face.

Karim gave a shout, but Naji pushed him towards the doorway. 'Get out.' And the two of them stumbled past, taking me with them.

Chapter Nine

I couldn't explain to Karim why Papi had acted that way. 'He didn't mean to scare you,' I said, but it made no difference. Karim stopped visiting our house.

In the weeks after Eid el Burbara, leading up to Christmas, Mami took us to church so many times that even the priest was tired of seeing us, and school blossomed into colour. Paper chains hung across classroom walls, tinsel was taped to the doors, and squares of painted aluminium foil glared from noticeboards. The lentils and chickpeas we'd been watering in cotton wool sprouted and were set in the manger round the brown-paper figures of Joseph and Mary, and schoolwork gave way to preparations for the Christmas play.

'Ruba,' called Mrs Atallah from the stage one afternoon, 'go and help Amal with her wings.' She waved to the side of the hall where a row of chairs was set out beneath the large windows. All alone on one of them, Amal sat curled up over a trail of white material.

'What?' I said, but Mrs Atallah had turned away to roll up a turban that had come undone.

My cow costume – a tail, horns and an old brown shirt that had belonged to Naji – was finished. I looked around for Karim but he wasn't there. His parents had said he couldn't be in the play, so he was helping to carry things on and off the stage. Ever since the night he'd seen her in the witch's window behind the face in the mist, we had avoided Amal. What had she been doing there? I didn't understand her, nobody did, yet now I had to walk across the hall and help her make angel's wings.

With every step, I moved further and further away from the children clustered near the stage. A sea of floorboard stretched out in front of me, and mountains sprouted behind as I went, cutting out the noise and putting miles between me and help. Dragging my tail behind me, I wished I was a Muslim too and not in the play.

The light fell on Amal's back, white as sugar, as I crossed the last mile of floorboard, and made a huge rectangle on the floor that hemmed us together. Standing beside her, I looked at the hair falling to her shoulders, straight and shiny like threads of black silk. Near her ear, a beautiful hairpin with a yellow and blue enamelled flower glistened in the sun. A pair of stiff white wings lay on her lap, a large needle plunging awkwardly in and out of them. The length of white material for the angel's skirt hung down in shiny folds over the side of the chair, and the black hair swung as the needle tugged and jabbed, making the wings twitch as though they were alive.

It was my feet she saw first. The needle stopped. Her eyes travelled up to my face.

I clutched my brown tail in both hands. My mouth was dry. 'Mrs Atallah said I had to help you.'

With the needle stuck halfway into the material, she stared – the questioning gaze I remembered from my birthday.

'She said I had to help you with the costume.'

Amal nodded.

Sitting down beside her, I glanced at the heart-shaped pieces of cardboard covered with cloth and white feathers and joined in the centre. One was bent.

Amal began again, her left hand holding the wings down as the right stitched them to the dress. She was barely halfway and already the wings seemed battered and dead.

'I – I can hold.'

The cow's tail slipped to the floor as I pulled a chair round. Reaching out, I slowly pressed down on the wings to hold them in place, and a moment later felt her fingers brush mine as she pulled the needle out and the cotton thread tightened.

Faint and far off near the stage there was a laugh and a shout. A girl giggled, and Mrs Atallah shouted impatiently at the boy with the turban, but in our spot beneath the window, the rectangle of light held us apart from the world.

A feather tickled my arm, reminding me of the chickens I'd let loose in the witch's yard. I was glad I'd done it: I had got back at her a little for what she'd done to Papi.

Amal bent down again and the metal point vanished in and out of the white cloth.

'You missed the wings!' I blurted.

I shouldn't have said it. The noise from the stage faded, or perhaps it was the light filling my ears. I waited, but Amal didn't pounce and my head didn't fall off. Only her big eyes made me uncomfortable.

'You've got to go to the left.' My mouth wouldn't stop flapping. 'To the left, not – not there. Shall I try? If you hold, I can try.'

She nodded.

I was careful not to touch her as I took the needle. But my hands wouldn't work with her so close beside me. Each stitch pointed in a different direction: one section was puckered tight, the next was loose.

I stitched upwards along the wings, away from her. Fast. The thread grew short before the end but I pulled it tight. 'It'll be enough,' I muttered. I didn't want to get another, to thread it under her gaze and spend even more time here.

It was her smile that made me lose my place: a sudden, unexpected smile that came from nowhere. It revealed two large front teeth with frilly bottoms. I had never seen them before, and they made the needle jerk.

It stabbed into her flesh a little above the knuckle. Stabbed in and stuck there, a fine point of silver and white light. Her watery eyes fixed on me. Then, still held by its thread, the needle fell out.

'I'm sorry,' I whispered from behind my fingers. 'I didn't do it on purpose.' Amal's finger made a bulge inside her cheek. 'I didn't mean it.'

A bang and a shout came from the far end of the hall, followed by laughter, but I didn't care about that. Amal was taking her finger out of her mouth. She didn't cry or make the slightest sound. Instead she reached up to her hair, drew out the enamelled pin and put it into my hand.

'Ghada, what do you know about Amal?' I didn't want to ask Papi or Mami, and Ghada knew everyone in Ein Douwra.

'Oh, that one,' she said. 'She lives up on the high road with her grandmother.'

'Her grandmother?'

Ghada was taking care of the shop today, and she put three more courgettes into a bag for me. 'What useless vegetables. What is there to do but stuff them with meat?'

The glass in the door shuddered as an explosion boomed. It seemed to come from everywhere.

'Burn their religion! My hair's going to turn white from nerves, and then who'll marry me? They're landing just down the road, I'll bet, and here I am in the shop. I might as well put a red flag on the roof so they can see more clearly where I am.'

'Missizbel's left,' I said. 'My teacher. She's gone back to *Scotlanda*.'

Ghada sighed and turned on her little radio. 'If only the rest of us could turn our arses to this country and fly off.'

'She says there's no shelling there.' I tried to imagine what it would be like, but couldn't. Perhaps Mami wanted to go somewhere like that, where things were so different she'd be happy the way she was in the photo.

Ghada shivered. It had snowed again last night, so heavily that the world was plugged up and hushed, and cars from higher up in the mountains crawled through Ein Douwra wearing tall hats of snow, many with chains wrapped round their tyres.

The air roared again, from further away this time, but we hardly noticed because a procession of hooting cars had turned off the main road and was streaming down the hill, the snow squeaking beneath their tyres.

Ghada stood watching at the door with a hand on her hip as they passed, their fronts, boots and door-handles decorated with flowers and ribbons. 'Which florist's responsible for such a tasteless arrangement, do you think? I wouldn't have accepted it for my wedding. Look – nothing but carnations, and half of them wilted. There's the bride.' Ghada pointed, then sank back against the doorframe. 'In any case, they could have done better with the flowers. Last week a beautiful one passed with lilies and roses. Even yesterday's funeral did better.' She clicked her tongue. 'You see how it is? One day they're laughing, the next they're crying. It's nothing but weddings and funerals these days.'

Back at the counter she wailed along to a song on the radio about 'true love' and some man holding your hand 'until it melted'. She seemed to think that would be a nice thing to happen.

'Any news from your uncle? Is he planning another visit?'

The image of the two men drinking coffee and talking in Jbeil flashed into my mind, but perhaps I'd been wrong. 'I don't know. But about Amal, some children at school think she can speak even though she never has, not even once.'

'Oh, that one had a voice all right – when her father tossed her here as if he were tossing out garbage, the shiftless good-for-nothing.' Ghada grunted scornfully.

'She had parents?' I exclaimed.

'What – then?'

'Where's her mother now?'

'Miss Yumna? Her parents married her off to that same good-for-nothing I was telling you about. An old man he was, compared to her. She didn't want to, of course. Who would?'

'Why not?'

'Because he wouldn't do a thing for a soul other than himself, that's why not. Wouldn't pee on your finger if it was

93

on fire. And he had wrinkles like an elephant, a head of dyed hair and half a dozen gold teeth to round off the picture. But he was rich, and that counts with a lot of people. It did with her parents. And money's no bad thing,' added Ghada, releasing another sigh into the shop. 'Now what else did your mother want?'

'Two kilos of tomatoes.'

She snapped a plastic bag off a metal hook. 'Tomatoes. You see what life has become? Life has become tomatoes.' She muttered to herself as she turned them over to make sure they were good. 'Here I am in the flower of my youth and I have to pick out other people's vegetables for them.'

Ghada lifted the bag onto the scale and the long needle shivered, then darted back to zero as she lifted it off again.

'Isn't Samira helping you?'

Ghada rolled her eyes. 'Every day it's something.'

'Is she sick?'

'That's what she says, but she'll outlive us all, you wait and see – unless they go and drop a bomb on us first. One day she hasn't the strength to eat, another she feels faint, and so it goes on. Last night, for instance, she couldn't sleep, so she had to keep everyone else awake too. Then at three in the morning she gets out of bed, makes a full *rakweh* of coffee, drinks the lot, comes back to bed and sleeps like a cow.'

I bent to pick a large tomato from the bag and cradled it in both hands. 'What happened to Amal's mother after she got married?'

Ghada whipped a metal file across her nails so that a tiny puff of nail-dust flew into the air. 'She came back for her father's funeral and never left.'

'You mean she's still up there?' A finger squished into the tomato.

'No, no, she's dead. When Miss Yumna died, there was only her husband's family left to bring up the child, but I suppose they couldn't be bothered any longer so she's been thrown here with her grandmother. But she had a voice back then, *ya haram*, before her mother died, that's what I remember.' She gave a mouth-shrug. 'It must have been the shock.'

I dropped the punctured tomato back into the crate. 'What did it sound like, her voice?'

Ghada lit a cigarette. 'Like a voice. What should a voice sound like?'

Chapter Ten

A few weeks after Christmas, Juhaina came by to ask Mami to a party, and I escaped to Teta's. Using both hands and with a cloth wrapped round her head, Teta was stirring her clothes in a large pot of steaming water with a wooden stick. The pot was in the bathtub, and the smell of hot soap rose with the steam. When she stopped stirring to pound the clothes, white cotton swelled into balls on the surface and was squashed down again.

I told Teta about Juhaina. 'She didn't go inside, just stayed in the kitchen. I don't think she likes Papi.'

'Will your mother go?'

'I'm not sure. She said no, but Juhaina said she must. She said she'd lend Mami a dress.'

I heard Juhaina's voice again. '*Soyons pratique*, Aida. You'll look nice, and no one will know.'

'Is it because we're poor?' I asked Teta.

She gave a scornful grunt. 'I've seen the way she goes into the shop, all dressed up in her fancy stuff, almost trailing a fur, and smiling as if the honey was dripping from her lips. And all the time talk talk talk, never stopping, like the bell on a mule's tail, and gathering gossip wherever she goes. That woman knows when a bird farts!'

My laughter made Teta chuckle softly to herself in that way she had, as if it was somewhere deep inside her. Then she started pounding and stirring the pot again.

'Teta, why do you wash that way?'

'I don't trust a machine to take the dirt out. In Africa the women used to go down to the river and wash their clothes there. They used a dried corncob to rub them. But this is the way my mother did it, and there's never a better way than your mother's.' She laid down the stick and wiped her forehead. 'Come, let me get you some food.'

She fetched a plateful of twisted cheese in syrup with a round of bread to the table. 'Eat, my soul, before you starve to death,' she said, pushing the plate towards me.

I pulled at a strand of cheese, which squeaked as I chewed it. A saucer of ash lay on the corner of the table. Another was in the kitchen and a third in Teta's bedroom. 'Incense,' she explained when I asked. 'I've been burning it every morning to cleanse the house. Maybe then the dreams will stop.'

Teta's hand was on the tabletop, the fingers curled like a brown flower.

'What kind of flowers were there in Africa, Teta?'

'In Nigeria? There were flowers, but not like here. I remember your grandfather bringing me a large pink one with petals as thin as tissue paper. He'd been fishing in the river, and most likely been drinking too. For the rest of his life he never remembered giving me that flower. *Ach*, how life was difficult there.'

'Why? Was there a war there too?'

'No. But we had nothing at first, no one did. That's why

we went out there. We kept a shop, and then the children came and had to be looked after.'

Jesus gazed down at me from his dinner table, at which everyone except him seemed to be talking. It was hard to believe that the plastic Virgin Mary on Teta's dresser was really his mother.

'Why did you go to Africa?'

'There was no work here. My brothers went first, God rest their souls, and they sent money so I could follow – all the way from our little village up in the north to Africa. We went in a boat. Fifteen years old, I was.'

'Didn't Jiddo go with you?'

'No. I met him there, in Africa. He was only a boy. He'd come over the same as me, working on a ship to pay his way. But what did any of us know about life?'

I took another bite of squeaky cheese. 'How did you get to marry him?'

She sighed. 'They brought us to him, the only two Lebanese girls in the village who weren't already married.'

'And did you like him from the first?'

'I liked him well enough – no more or less than I liked anyone else – but no, *habibti*, it was him who wanted to marry.' She tutted. 'What did I want with marriage? But there was no choice. A woman needs a husband, doesn't she? Even if he was as young and scrawny as your grandfather.' She gave a little laugh. 'So they brought us to him. He looked first at me, then at the other woman, and shrugged. "Doesn't matter which," he said, but he looked longest at me, so that was it. We got married. After your grandfather had chosen, we spoke, that other woman and I. "God gave me big teeth," she said, and she wasn't wrong. "And so my life will be different from yours: difficult. Difficult because I have big teeth. That's why the boy chose you and not me." I don't know whether it was true, but maybe it was.'

'Didn't she ever get married, then?'

Teta smiled. 'Oh, she got married. There wasn't anyone for her at first – there weren't so many of us Lebanese out there – but later on others arrived. She married a man your grandfather knew from round these parts. Perhaps he didn't care about her teeth. And of course he was poorer even than us. By that time your grandfather missed this country so much we came back, but she and her husband stayed. They didn't come back till years later, and by the time they did, he was a rich man.'

'Did he come back to Ein Douwra?'

'Of course. Men never leave their village. They always come back. It's only the women who must leave.'

She fell to smoothing the plastic tablecloth, running her hand across it until it couldn't get any flatter.

'Don't you miss your village, Teta?'

Her hand grew still. 'I think of my village and our house every day. Every day I think of my mother, who didn't come to Africa with us.'

Outside, the snow had melted and the cold had begun to fade away. A breeze moved the branches of the trees.

'Teta, that man, the rich one, where does he live?'

Her left arm rose. 'They used to live up there, but that was years ago. He died. Now only his wife is left, up at the old house on the bend in the high road.'

'The house on the bend?'

'It was beautiful back then, with a garden at the front, and a fountain, the only house in the area that had one.

The children used to come from miles around just to look.'

I thought of Amal: Amal who wasn't so awful any more, just strange. Glancing up at the painting on the wall, I wondered what Jesus's voice had sounded like. High- or low-pitched? Complaining like Samira's, or soft and buttery like Uncle's? Did Jesus whistle through his nose as he breathed the way the Rose Man did, or didn't he talk much at all like Papi and Naji?

Teta shook her head. 'We used to be friends once, that woman and I, and our children played together.'

'Papi and Uncle Wadih?'

'Yes, they knew her. And her daughter too, God rest her soul. But then . . .' Teta stopped and her face darkened. 'And look at him now. Look what kind of a life he leads. All because of her.' She pushed back her chair and stood up.

'You mean Papi?' I asked.

'Eat, eat, my heart,' she said as she left the room.

But I couldn't eat any more. Teta must have meant Papi. She knew who was responsible for the way he was, just like I did. She knew he'd been cursed, and that was why she had stopped being friends with the witch. But a minute later I thought of something else, something that made the cheese sit heavy in my stomach. I pushed back my chair and rushed off to find Naji. I had to tell him.

He wasn't at home. 'He's gone to play in the forest,' Mami said, so I ran down the hill.

The forest had changed. Apart from several new craters where bombs had landed, the leaves had fallen off bushes, and flowers had died away. Only the pines remained, upright and unchanged.

I was still searching for Naji when a bright colour between the trees caught my eye: Ali coming down the path, looking special in a red shirt. He wasn't standing upright, though, but bent and walking slowly as if he was searching for something.

'Is the roastery closed?' I called.

His head snapped up. Then he grinned and came over. He looked big even for a grown-up as he clumped through the trees, his thick body topped by a solid head with sticking-out ears.

'It's my afternoon off.' His scalp showed through wet comb lines.

'What were you looking for?'

'Looking for?'

'Just then, over there.'

Ali stared at the ground. 'Nothing.' His hands burrowed deep into his pockets. 'I . . . lost something before.'

'What?' I asked, but Ali sucked in his lips and wouldn't say. 'Do you come to the forest a lot?' I went on. 'I've never seen you here before.'

'I come early in the morning before work, when the forest's new.'

'There's Naji!' I cried. Between the trees, I saw him whacking the earth with a stick, and ran ahead, bursting to tell him my thought. 'If it wasn't for her big teeth, the witch could have been our grandmother!'

Naji scowled. 'What are you talking about?'

I explained quickly, but after scratching his head a little, Naji went back to hitting and poking the ground.

'But she could have been!' I insisted. 'Don't you want to ask her about it?'

'No.'

I glared. 'You never want to do anything any more.'

He continued flicking earth out of a hole, his face pursed tightly. 'Don't be such a baby, there's no such thing as witches.'

It was as though he'd shoved me away. Why didn't he agree with me any more? Suddenly I felt small.

Ali came up behind me. 'They were talking in the shop about the witch,' he whispered. 'They said someone let her chickens out, and they got stolen or eaten by dogs.'

'Good! She's an evil old witch and she deserves everything she gets.'

'Yes.' Ali nodded seriously, then peered down at something. 'Look,' he said, squatting beside a cyclamen that had begun to push out of the soil. 'God dropped it here.'

'Can you see everything?' I asked. 'I mean because your eyes point different ways.'

'I don't see anything out of this one.' A finger rose to his left eye and he shut the right, just to make sure. 'No, nothing. But I can see everything I need to see. And from up in the roastery I can see the whole world.' He touched the cyclamen gently with a finger. 'It's still too small to squeeze it so it pees on your hand.'

'That's not pee,' Naji commented as he whipped the flaky bark off a tree. 'It's yellow powder.'

'It *is* pee,' said Ali. 'Flower's pee.'

'Don't be so stupid,' said Naji, then stopped. 'I didn't mean—' He flushed and Ali looked upset.

'It *is* pee,' I agreed, to make Ali feel better.

Naji snorted. 'Fine. Then you're as stupid as he is.'

'What's wrong with him?' whispered Ali.

'He's angry,' I replied, because he was. He seemed that way a lot of the time now.

'Yes.' Ali nodded, chewing his thumb. 'Angry.'

A rumble like thunder made Naji come alive. 'Explosives!' He leapt up.

Ali wiped his forehead the way he always did, even though he wasn't in the roastery and there was no sweat there now. 'Let's go back,' he said.

'Don't you want to see what that was?' Quickly, Naji led us a different way through the forest until we reached a place where the trees sloped steeply into the valley. He jerked his chin towards the bottom of the mountainside. 'They've got big diggers.' Tractors lined the road below the forest, and clouds of dust rose from the earth. Beside the road, the mountain had been sliced away in red and white gashes.

'Is that what the sound was?' said Ali.

Naji nodded. 'It's for stones to make buildings with so the Beirutis can come up here and hide. They blow up the mountain.'

Ali's face puckered. 'Are they killing it?' He took hold of my sleeve. 'Are they, Ruba?'

But I didn't know. 'What if they reach here to our forest?'

'Then it'll all collapse!' Naji's arms rose. '*Boom!*'

'It'll be gone? Our forest?'

Ali put out his hand and started stroking my hair, his hand moving light as water over my head, but it didn't help. I had a pain in my chest at the thought.

Chapter Eleven

There was silence in the house. School had been closed for two days because of the shelling, but now it was quiet. There had been an argument between Mami and Papi when she'd told him about the party, and she'd gone to open the shop. Naji was at a friend's house, and Papi was asleep in his chair.

I tiptoed into the living room to watch him. He was slumped sideways, one hand holding his forehead. The other lay in his lap, its fingers pointing up like a dead thing on its back – pointing towards his face, which hung heavy with two creases between the brows, eyes squeezed shut as if he were making a wish. On the floor, his feet in their black leather slippers were still as rocks.

At first I watched from the doorway, then from the island of the rug, creeping along the pattern lines, toe to heel, toe to heel, until I was beside the chair nearest to his. One more step and I could reach him. A single hop and I was touching the armrest.

He was as soft and harmless as wet dough. The spiky thoughts that pricked him from inside had gone and left him full of dreams. Papi with his rigid nerves, tight muscles and craziness that had scared Karim was no longer in that floppy body: he'd flown out of the open hand and gone somewhere else. His head, usually so heavy with thoughts, drooped against the worn patch of fabric.

The window showed grains of light in the air around us, tiny glowing specks that floated at their own speed. I heard no sound but the bump of my heart, which seemed to have risen into my head, and everywhere there were brilliant full stops of light. It reminded me of Amal: the chair, the light, and the deep, deep silence.

There was no stopping now. Next to the hand on his forehead, the spilt vinegar mark was pulling my finger towards it. If it could only be wiped away. And he was asleep the way they slept in stories, for a hundred years, magical sleeps that nothing could shake. Nothing was going to wake Papi now: not a shout, a scream, a jump or a shake, and certainly not the touch of a finger. In the middle of the drowsy air he slept, a king on his throne surrounded by sprinkles of sun-gold. Even the room was asleep, corked up and stilled.

My finger moved through the silence towards him. And suddenly, in the hollowness of the house, it was clear that I was going to wipe off that mark and free him; wake him up into the person he used to be. He would move and rub his eyes, blink a few times, then with a smile he would get up and—

It was like pressing a button. The dead thing in his lap became a hand again, sprang up alive and bit me hard. It held my wrist so I couldn't move.

The king had woken, his eyes popping open. Then Papi returned from wherever he'd been, rigid inside his body, his neck stiff, a thick red line dented into his head where his hand had been.

The light falling in through the window faded. The specks of gold were gone. I waited for him to grow crazy the way he had been when he saw the Burbara mask, and my wrist hurt as I tried to pull it loose.

'What are you doing?' His voice was curled up tight.

I pulled my hand again, but the fingers round my wrist were made of metal.

'Nothing. I wasn't doing anything.'

The black eyes searched my face, didn't move, weren't even a little sleepy.

'I was . . . I wanted to touch the mark . . . on your head.'

His hand fell away from mine and he leant back. The creases between his eyebrows returned. 'What for?'

The silences in the house whirled round us like water. It was strange standing so close to him. 'To take it away.'

He looked surprised: not crazy, just surprised.

'Papi?'

'Yes?'

'If you cut a salamander's tail off, will it grow back again?' The question came from the back of my mind where it had been hiding until this moment.

'No. Why do you ask?'

'A boy at school did it. Sliced the tail off one.'

For a moment the face in front of me was pained. 'They mutilate animals the same way they do men in this country. You see the men who have lost their limbs – you see them in the streets, don't you? But there are others, Ruba, others who have had their spirits and hearts and souls amputated.'

I watched the ropes on his neck. 'What's "amputated"?'

'It means "cut off".'

I thought a moment. Could someone's voice get amputated? A voice, cut off. It would be floating out there in space where no one could hear it.

The black eyes searched mine. 'And this boy, what he did, you saw this?'

I nodded, and he looked worried. 'Children are resilient,' he murmured. Then he looked up, his mouth more relaxed. 'So you were going to take the mark on my head away, were you? And how were you going to do that, *ha*, Ruba?'

'I was going to rub it off.'

The slippered feet unglued themselves from the floor. The chair creaked as he leant forwards. '*Yalla*, then. Go on. Rub it off.' The forehead was in front of me, the spilt vinegar mark with its wavy edges standing out like a mistake on a page.

I rubbed with one finger, then two. Then I made a fist and tried with that. But the stain was still there.

'Do you want to go and get your rubber?' Papi sat back. 'That makes you laugh, *ha*?' He smiled at me, but soon the smile turned sad. 'And if it works, your magic rubber that can wipe things from my head, you can lend it to me.'

'Why?' The house was still and full of nothing. 'What do you want to rub out, Papi?'

No answer came, only the black eyes stared through me now at something else.

'Papi, they're breaking up the mountain down in the forest and taking it away.'

'Fools without brains!' He heaved a big breath. 'They're digging up forests all over Lebanon, Ruba, not only here, wiping out our land. They're even quarrying the caves in Nahr el Kalb, destroying treasures of archaeology that will

107

never come again. Using the caves at J'eeta as ammunition stores – caves that if they were abroad would be protected night and day for their beauty. And now our officials take bribes from foreign countries so they can bury their poisonous waste in our land or dump it in our sea. Do you think anyone cares about nature, about the future? All they care about is money.'

He sank into his thoughts.

'Papi, there's something else.'

He blinked. 'What? More questions?' The half-nod meant I could go ahead and ask.

'Naji's growing quiet. He doesn't talk to me much any more. Is that the way people get when they grow older?'

'What, silent?'

'Yes.' Then I remembered something. 'Uncle said there's no such thing as silence. He said that every silence says something: the silences between words, between notes in music and between people.'

'Perhaps he's right.'

We sat there, listening to the silence. Then Papi pulled himself out of his chair.

'Where are you going?'

'To find your mother.'

It didn't take him long to put on his shoes and leave. Next to me, his chair was empty for the first time in weeks. Just now he'd talked to me, been soft with me, smiled at me. And it wasn't only him: everyone was different. Naji didn't want to be with me. Amal wasn't scary any more. And the witch: Naji said there were no such things. And if she had a granddaughter and used to be Teta's friend . . . but, no, Teta had admitted that it was the witch who'd changed Papi. 'Look what kind of a life he leads,' she'd said. 'All because of her.'

I looked at Papi's empty chair. He'd let me touch his scar, answered my questions, made me laugh. Yes, everything seemed to be changing. It was a strange sensation, as if everything was connected and I couldn't see how. Suddenly I wanted to sit in his chair. Maybe if I sat in it I would understand.

Taking a good look to make sure he wasn't coming back, I stepped up to it. The brown threads had come loose in places – the armrests, the headrest, the cushion where Papi's legs pressed – so that the yellowing sponge underneath showed through. None of the other chairs or the sofa looked so old.

Slowly, I eased myself onto it and settled back. But it wasn't comfortable. It had taken on too much of his shape, as if it were part of him. His thighs had dented the fabric, and the chair was filled with his ghost. The rounds of his bottom were there too, and the cup shape made by his head. The armrests had worn away – the places where his fingers had pinched and rubbed and gripped, the spot where his elbow rested as he read the paper or worried his new string of beads; a hole on the right where he had picked out the sponge without thinking. And the patches below my hanging feet where the carpet had been scraped thin from the inch-movements of his slippers.

This was the place where he sat, and slept sometimes, his head fallen back, jaw slightly sunk, the throat-bone a tiny mountain stippled with hairs, his fingers laced on his stomach as if they were cupping a secret.

The room looked funny from this angle, different from what it really was. The kitchen doorway was on the far side of the dining room, just the corner of the counter in sight. Mami moved backwards and forwards all the time in there: he could see her, or bits of her. We came in that way too, leaving footsteps that Mami cleaned behind us, the wet floor glimmering in summer. Teta's stories came in, carried by us, floated into the room and out again as Naji and I passed through, running, bleeding, crying, laughing, carrying schoolbags out, then throwing them down at the end of the day. We cast looks across the room at the chair, looks that were sometimes curious and sometimes frightened. Meals were eaten, the television switched on and off, and life moved round again the next day.

I saw things from the chair that I had never seen from anywhere else: a crack in the corner of the ceiling opposite, the way the light fell so you could see the new dust on the coffee-table even though Mami had dusted today. The vase of artificial flowers looked more artificial from here, the pink, red, yellow and orange plastic ridged, the leaves that hadn't yet been pulled out hanging loose on the stems. The sofa was threadbare where we sat on it, with a loganberry-cordial stain that had been my fault.

Cars passed outside: our car clanking and whining as it took us to school, Uncle's car, followed by screams and yells of joy. Ghada and Samira's footsteps sounded often on the stairs outside the window, and the slower ones of the Rose Man too when he came down to water his roses and speak lovingly to them. Rollerskates whizzed up and down, Karim and I called to each other outside. And in the kitchen the clatter of cutlery and plates, the chopping, stirring and wiping. And occasionally the faint humming of a song.

A fly landed on the armrest and, lowering my face, I saw its crusty, varnished lace wings and the hairs that stood out on its body, thicker on the jointed legs that had hooks for feet. Perhaps it saw me too out of its huge eyes. It walked, start, stop, start, stop, feeling its way with the long straw that hung out of its mouth, and when it stopped, it soaped its hands together like Uncle.

I brought both knees to my chin and dug my hands under me between the seat cushion and the chair's wooden frame so I could think. There were metal springs beneath the fabric, I could feel the hard circles. But there was something else too. Something crinkly, with edges.

I took hold and slid it out. It was an envelope, and looked as if it had been under there for a long time. I turned it over. It wasn't sealed, so I took out what was inside. There were three sheets of paper covered with Papi's curly handwriting. I read the first side. The writing started off neat, then turned messy and hurried.

Age: 6 to 8 years
Height: small, not yet chest-high
Hair: long and brown
Eyes: brown
Clothes: flip-flops and a dress, couldn't tell what colour
Chipped red polish on her left thumbnail where she'd been sucking it. She was old to be still sucking her thumb. And the rest of her was covered in sand and dirt – hair, arms, legs. It was on her eyelashes, round her mouth, and in the single crease on her throat. She was nothing but a girl made of dust.

That was all that was written on the first page. Before I could look at the second, I heard footsteps in the kitchen. I had just time to fold the pages and tuck them behind me.

'What are you doing?' Naji was staring at me from the kitchen doorway.

'Nothing. Just – just trying Papi's chair out.'

From here, Naji looked far away. He stayed a minute not saying anything, then scowled and carried on into his room.

Suddenly the chair was uncomfortable. Sitting in it, I had told my first lie to Naji.

Still holding the envelope, I slipped off the chair. And as my feet touched the floor I realized how much I wanted Papi back. Standing there gazing at it, the chair became covered in warm light again. It seemed to reassure me that spells, no matter what sort they were, could be broken.

Chapter Twelve

A few days later, Teta sent us out to hunt for snails in the scrub above the main road. It had been raining, and as twilight started to fall, Naji, Karim and I squatted with our plastic bags and picked snails from the grass and the undersides of leaves. We followed trails of silver up tree-trunks and across stones, found the smooth coiled shells of brown threaded with grey and plopped them into our bags. I liked the way the snails' bodies stuck out of the shell – their sticky bottoms, and the antennae that Karim said were eyes and that shrank back fast when you touched them.

As I searched, I couldn't stop thinking about the envelope I'd found under Papi's chair cushion. I'd kept it and read it a dozen times. At first I thought the girl he'd written about was me, but I didn't look like that. My hair was black, I didn't suck my thumb, and had never been covered from head to toe in dust. So whoever she was, that girl wasn't me. The other two pages made even less sense. At the top of the first was a heading, 'Places Searched', above a list of areas of Beirut with addresses, each one crossed through. The second page was 'People Asked', and another list, this time of names, again each with a line through it. No matter how many times I read those three pages, they didn't make sense. I wanted to ask Papi what it all meant but I couldn't, and I wasn't sure yet whether to say anything about it to Mami or Teta, or even to Naji.

Soon the bottom of my plastic bag was a frothing, clicking mass, and so was Karim's, but Naji had hardly any because he was hunting for more than just snails. A few days ago he'd come home dragging a metal canister. He had pulled it into his bedroom, sweat dripping from his face.

I examined it from all angles. 'What is it?'

It stood there in the corner of the room, almost as tall as I was, painted white and brown, with numbers and letters along one side. I tried to move it but it was heavy. And the top of the thing looked odd – shaped like some sort of wheel.

'That's the lid.' Naji turned it hard, then lifted it off and laid it on the floor.

I peered inside. 'There's nothing here,' I announced, my voice hollow.

He sighed. 'Of course not. They don't need it any more. It was used to store artillery shells, but now it's mine.'

'What do you want it for?'

He stood a little taller. 'I'm going to collect shells and fill it right to the top.'

'Shells?'

'From the woods. There are loads of them everywhere. The soldiers leave all sorts of bullets and things.'

That day he found two torn red cylinders with copper-coloured bottoms, each with a little circle in the middle. A few days later there were more: thin cylinders of shiny silver or gold that softened into rounded points at one end.

There were big versions and little versions, mostly dented, but he found some that were like new.

I unglued a huge snail from a stone and dropped it into my bag. 'Is Papi really going to eat these?'

Naji shrugged. 'Who cares what he does?'

A moment later he found another of the coloured plastic cylinders, but he tossed it to one side.

'Why are you throwing it away?'

'I've already got lots of those.'

It wasn't long before he found a pretty gold one.

'I like those best,' I told him. I liked to weigh them in my hands, like large beads, or line them up end to end, or fit the small ones into the larger ones, if they were empty, or clink them together.

'Where are you going?'

Naji was wandering off. 'You stay and hunt for snails if you want,' he said.

'Are you going to look for more bullets?' I called, but there was no answer as he disappeared through the trees.

Not long afterwards the thunder of shelling started, so Karim and I headed towards home.

The sound of bombing bounced between the hills in screeches and bangs as we walked along the main road. Karim was trying to get a whistle out of a blade of grass held between his thumbs. He filled himself up with breath and gave a big puff. Nothing. Instead, we heard laughter coming from a narrow path to the right. A plane passing high up spread a roaring noise across the sky, making two cats jump down from some rubbish drums and dart away. But as the roar faded the laughter came again.

'Let's not stop,' said Karim. 'I don't like those boys.'

A small group was clustered a little way down the path beside a bent telegraph pole. There were three boys. Two of them – one with heavy-lidded green eyes and another with spots all over his face – were older. But it was the sight of the third boy that made me stop. Because it was Naji.

The green-eyed one was rubbing something metallic and shiny against his sleeve, while a rounded piece of wood stuck out from beneath his armpit. It was only when he moved that the wood and the metal blended together and I knew what it was.

'See the handle? Here's where you open it,' he explained to Naji. The metal stem of the rifle fell downwards, hanging like a broken limb. 'And here's where you put the bullets in.'

Karim's blade of grass fluttered to the ground as he tugged my arm. 'Let's go. They might shoot us if we don't.'

I shook him off. 'Shoot us? What are you talking about? Can't you see Naji's with them?'

The rifle clicked, the broken limb knitted together again, and the boy holding it leant against the twisted railings behind him. Dirty brown knees stuck out beneath his shorts. One sock was pulled halfway up his calf, the other sagged round his ankle.

'Look.' He raised the rifle to his shoulder and swept the metal end through the air until it was pointing at the nearest pine tree. The boys fell still. Naji stood with both hands locked on top of his head, his elbows jutting out like roast chicken wings.

With a loud crack, a branch on the tree shook, and the green-eyed boy jerked back against the railings.

'Let me try!' cried Naji. 'I want a go!' His arms were stretched out towards the gun, but the boy swung it clear.

'Ruba!' Karim's voice was insistent. 'Let's go.'

Perhaps the gun-boy heard him, because the rifle swept round, away from Naji's groping hands, to where I was standing. Two black holes in the tip of the rifle-stem faced me like eyes.

The boys seemed suddenly far away. Among them, Naji's face stood out, shocked and afraid. Then the rifle's small black eyes grew large – became Amal's eyes, Papi's, watching from a place that was dark and silent.

'Hey! Hey, be careful. That's my sister!'

The world started to move again, and Naji's face grew close. The others' too.

The rifle quivered, and behind it the green-eyed boy gave a casual shrug. The gun was lowered. 'I wasn't going to do anything.'

Naji pushed his way past and ran up. 'What are you doing here?' he hissed. 'And him.' He jerked his head towards Karim. 'Go home.'

'No. Who are those two?'

'My friends. And it's nothing to do with you.'

As he spoke, his friends stepped up.

'What's this?' asked the spotty one. 'Your little sister?'

'Isn't she cute?' laughed the gun-boy. 'And the other – he's going to piss in his pants!'

They laughed. Naji laughed too. The smile was still on his lips when he whispered, '*Yalla*, go home.'

'If I go back I'll tell Mami – or Papi! – and then you'll see.'

'Ohhhh, she's going to tell Papi,' mimicked the spotty one.

There were hoots of laughter, and two red stains spread across Naji's cheeks.

'And what about this one?' The spotty boy indicated Karim, whose eyes were enormous with fear. 'I know you. You're a Muslim, aren't you?' He gave Karim a shove.

'Yes,' said Naji. 'He is.'

'What's in your bags? Let's have a look.' The gun-boy came closer and tugged at Karim's . 'Snails! Ohhh, you've been out collecting snails like good little children, have you?'

Naji stood watching, and I noticed that he didn't have his bag any more.

'Is that what you Muslims eat, then? Filthy slimy snails? Bet you eat them raw too.'

'They're not mine,' said Karim.

'No, of course they're not.'

'They aren't! They're hers!' He held out his bag against my chest so I had to take it. But they didn't leave him alone.

'You're not one of us,' said the spotty boy, 'so what are you doing here in our town?'

'He's a snivelling puny little coward,' said the gun-boy. He glanced at Naji. 'Isn't that right?'

Naji nodded. 'They've split Beirut to keep them apart from us. We should split Ein Douwra as well to keep them away.'

'Naji!' I cried.

The gun-boy lowered his rifle to the floor and leant on it the way the Rose Man leant on his stick. 'Go home. Run and tell Papi, little one,' he mocked, pinching my cheek and ruffling my hair.

'Get off!' I shouted, but couldn't push him away because I was carrying a bag in each hand now.

I turned and started to run, but gravel slid under my feet and the ground came up to meet me. There was a crunch as the bags of snails hit the ground.

Laughter rose like a flock of birds.

As I picked myself up and stumbled away, Karim's footsteps pattered after me. My knee burnt where a flap of skin hung loose, and blood trickled down my leg.

Karim stopped outside his building, but I ran on.

It was dark indoors, and I could tell from the silent fridge that the electricity had been cut. I dropped the bags on the kitchen floor and stopped in the dining room to catch my breath.

Raised voices came from behind the living-room door.

'How long has it been since you took an interest in the children or in their upbringing? Or in anything at all?' came Mami's voice. 'It's me who's left to do all that. And nothing changes: today could be yesterday for all I can tell. It could be last week, or a year ago. Nothing changes, do you hear?'

'In God's name, what do you expect when the country's being torn apart, when you can't put on the radio or pick up a paper without a reminder?'

'Don't you dare talk about God! What have you to do with God? What have you to do with anything?'

'Is that why you went out the other night with that woman?'

A few nights ago Mami had come out of her room looking like someone else in a green dress and a golden belt. Her hair was done in a different way, and she was wearing red lipstick. I'd been scared that she'd enjoy herself so much she wouldn't come back.

'That woman's my friend,' replied Mami.

'But going out to parties alone?'

'Because *you* wouldn't come with me!'

'A married woman by herself! What will people think?'

119

'I don't care what they think. Or what you think. I can't remember the last time I stepped out of this house unless it was to open the shop or buy food or take and fetch the children. I can't remember the last time I sat down and talked to another human being.'

The living-room door swung open. Mami's face was quivering, and a tea-towel was stretched taut between her hands. She went down the hall and their bedroom door closed behind her. In the gloom, I could make out Papi standing in the middle of the living room.

With a snap the electricity came on. There was a click and a whirr from the kitchen as the fridge started up. Bright light flooded the living room, and Papi stood blinking at me with a desperate expression.

It was half an hour before Naji came home. I heard him go into his room, then come out again and pause outside my door. He pushed it open. In his arms was a stack of comics, which he set down on the chest of drawers. 'You can read these if you want. I've finished them.'

Still sitting on the bed hugging my knees, I continued looking out of the window.

'Does your knee hurt?'

'Go. Away.'

He ran his thumb up and down one corner of the pile of comics so they made a flicking sound.

'They weren't being mean on purpose. Those two older ones are already in the militia. They're grown up enough to fight, and soon I will be as well.' His face brightened, but only for an instant. 'You didn't tell Papi, did you?'

I didn't answer.

'You mustn't say anything. You mustn't tell either of them. Swear you won't.'

'They made fun of Karim, you all did; and that one with the funny eyes nearly killed me.'

Naji rubbed the back of his neck. 'Don't tell them.'

I thought about it. 'Promise you won't play with those boys again.'

His nostrils flared. 'No!'

I stared out of the window again. 'Fine.'

Daylight was fading, and across the street a light came on.

Naji spoke quietly. 'If I promise, then you won't tell Mami and Papi?'

I nodded.

He took a deep breath. 'All right,' he said. 'All right, I promise.'

Chapter Thirteen

When I saw Karim at school, he wasn't angry with me, only with Naji because he turned his back when he saw him. We didn't talk about what had happened. Karim seemed to want to forget about it, and I didn't care if he was a Muslim or not. To me he was just Karim. Besides, I had other things to worry about.

All week I dreamt of stump-tailed salamanders, snails with cracked shells and girls covered in dust. Most often, though, I dreamt of chickens. They limped and flapped their wings, squawking in pain, feathers flecked with blood. And their eyes, unblinking and surrounded by scaly red skin, looked at me accusingly. Each morning I felt worse and worse about what I'd done, until, after waking from another chicken dream, I decided to tell Teta.

She was on the balcony repotting young plant shoots into bigger containers, 'so they can breathe'. When I told her I'd let those chickens out and Ali said they'd been killed, she looked at me hard until I squirmed. Then she handed me a container to repot, and I worked in silence, the soil black and bitter between my fingers.

Gathering the spilt soil on the floor into a mound, Teta scooped it up and patted it down round the young shoots, then pushed the tin into the corner so it could catch the sun. Her lips were pursed tight as she took up a broom and swept.

'You can come up there with me and apologize,' she said at last, banging the broom against the wall to release the soil.

'What?' My dirty fingers tingled. 'We can't! You're not friends with her any longer.'

'Well,' she said slowly, 'we were friends once, and it's time I let the skin heal over my anger.'

'But we can't go there! What about . . . what about the curse?'

Teta turned round. 'What curse?'

'The one she put on Papi.'

It took Teta a moment, then she gave a shuddering laugh. 'But you said she did!'

'Me? I never said any such thing, child.'

I stared. Teta never lied.

She gave the broom one last thump against the wall. 'Go and wash your hands. We're leaving in a few minutes.'

The further up the hill we got, the heavier Teta's breathing became. By the time we turned into the narrow lane that ran further uphill past the nut shop, she was puffing like a runner.

The smell of hot sugar came from a fan in the wall, and I looked up to see if Ali was there to throw me down some sugared almonds, but today there was no face behind the metal grille.

The lane was longer and steeper than it had ever been before. A car came down slowly with a skidding of tyres, braking, releasing, then braking again. Finally we got to the top and walked along the dusty edge of the high road. I would have slowed as we drew near the witch's house, but Teta had me by the hand.

The front yard was quiet. It looked different in the daylight: just a sandy yard, with a sad broken fountain in its centre. A watery shade was cast by the three trees Karim and I had crept under and, with a guilty pang, I saw there were only two white chickens scratching and pecking the ground now.

'It used to be the richest house in the area,' muttered Teta, shaking her head as we walked towards the mesh door.

We stopped on the step and Teta stood biting her lip and frowning. Finally she knocked on the wooden frame. Through the fine mesh, it was dark inside.

My sweaty hand slid out of Teta's grasp as I half turned, undecided whether to run and save myself or stay and protect Teta. One of the chickens squawked softly. A leaf floated down and settled with a whisper on the dry ground.

A shuffling sound came from inside and Teta shifted her weight from one leg to the other. Then someone appeared in the square of light on the other side of the mesh door: a pair of feet in worn slippers, and the skirt of a dress with buttons down the front, the faded material scattered with small yellow and blue flowers. It stood there alone, half a body in the light. It was her.

The half a body had an old woman's voice with a country accent. 'Who's there?'

The door creaked open. The top hinge was broken, making it hang out once it came away from the frame, like a loose tooth that needed just one good tug. The hand that held it open was old, and as wide and rough as the feet. Then the body grew whole: a head with a cotton cloth wrapped round it, a face hundreds of years old, older even than Teta's, and eyes closed narrow against the sunlight. Below them, the mouth was crowded round with lines, a purse that had had its string pulled tight.

She looked at me, then at Teta.

'Latifeh,' Teta said. That was all; just the name.

'You?' The wrinkled face eased a little. The one good hinge creaked. 'Is it you come to visit me after all these years? After all this time?'

Teta nodded. 'Our grandchildren play together now. They go to school together and the past is forgotten. And us: what do we want with the past?'

We were still alive on our side of the door, on that stone step in the sunshine with the two chickens scratching and muttering at our backs.

Then the thick body moved aside – 'Come in, *ahlan*' – and Teta pulled me with her. We were in a large kitchen, cool and dim with a stone floor. A lightbulb hung from the ceiling above a plastic-topped table with scorchmarks where pots had been set down, and scratches where a knife had cut. Paint flaked off the walls, like ancient skin, and there was a brown patch where the rain had come through.

'Amal! Where are you, *ya* Amal?'

There was a bang from the back of the house, running feet, and Amal came in, stumbling to a halt beside the table. Her eyebrows closed together when she saw me, but then she smiled: a smile so big her face cracked open.

The witch's hand ran over Amal's head and rested on her shoulder. It was a strange thing, that old shaking hand lying

125

on the clean red and white dress with its lacy collar. 'Is this your friend, my soul?'

Amal came and took my arm, and we followed the grown-ups out of the kitchen and into an echoing room that had a sofa covered with a blue sheet, a table with four wooden chairs, a sideboard with a stack of plates in it, and two pictures on the wall. Teta and the witch sat on the sofa.

Beside me hung a picture of Jesus and angels shooting out light, and next to it, a black-and-white photograph: a man and woman leaning against a shiny car. The man's moustache was curled up at either end, and the woman wore a fancy dress and jewels even though she wasn't pretty. It was hard to tell whether she was smiling or not, she had such big teeth.

Amal let go of my arm and went to pick up a plastic doll from the floor. It had long ragged hair, and eyes that swung open and shut as it was tilted.

'What shall I offer you?' the witch asked Teta. 'Coffee? Something to eat?'

'No, nothing.'

The offer came again, but still Teta refused.

Amal fetched the doll and handed it to me. I took it, although I was too old for such things.

'So many years it's been. So many,' said the witch. 'But nothing's changed, except birth and death. Life has been a circle, and here I am, back where I started, poor and alone, if it weren't for this child. And what I remember is not my life but someone else's.'

'Someone else's?' asked Teta.

'You see that picture on the wall? That's my husband. And who's standing next to him? You think that woman is me?' The witch laughed drily. 'No. Pockets weighed down with money suck the brains out of a person till they're no longer themselves.'

I made myself look away from that creased face. Thinking about it would make it happen: she would suddenly be full of life, ready to jump up and catch me in her arms, in her mouth with its big teeth.

'*Ach.*' Teta sighed. 'And here we are without husbands again, just like the day we met, and with even more troubles on our heads. When we were young we didn't have such troubles, not before the men came.'

As I held the doll, Amal plaited its hair, left over right, right over left, and with each pull, the long-lashed eyes winked at me.

The witch spoke now. 'Did he . . . ?'

'Yes, he passed away.'

She rubbed her scarved head. 'That's right, I remember now. I remember. How many years is it?'

'Eleven, God rest his soul. We knew he had a weak heart, it runs in his family, but even when you know it's coming, you're never prepared.'

'I don't remember what happened yesterday – whether the sun rose and sank, whether I ate or drank – but him, standing there trying to pick out a wife, that I'll never forget.'

'He was a scrawny thing, wasn't he? Scrawny as a half-plucked chicken, and so young it wasn't certain whether it was a wife he needed or a straw to drink his milk through.' Teta laughed inside her chest, and another deeper laugh joined hers.

'God bless him.'

Amal had finished plaiting and, tossing the doll on the floor again, pulled me through the kitchen into the yard.

There I could breathe again. 'Have you got any chalk? We can play hopscotch. Do you know hopscotch?'

She shook her head.

'I'll show you. Have you got a piece of chalk?'

She shook her head again. Then she thought a moment and ran back inside. I sat down on the stone step to wait. The sun seemed close and shone down in splintered threads of metal. The chickens' claws raked through the sand, a lizard slipped down the house wall like water, and wavy patterns of light shifted on the ground beneath the nearest tree. Small fruit peeped out from among its leaves: white mulberries.

The screen door banged and Amal reappeared with a green wax crayon. I took it and drew hopscotch squares on the flagstones in front of the kitchen, then numbered them. 'We need a stone now.'

Amal found one, and I showed her how to play. Soon we were hopping from square to square, and carried on until a call came from the kitchen.

'Amal, where are you?'

We found Teta sitting at the table picking mint off the stem. There were two piles of stalks, but now the witch was standing near the sink making a sandwich. A moment later she rolled up the bread and cut it in half. 'Here. Eat, eat.' As she gave one half to me and the other to Amal, I noticed her hands were shaking. 'What's your name, my girl?'

The sandwich was squished tight in my fist. 'Ruba.'

'Ruba. Yes, Ruba.'

I glanced at Teta for some sign of what I should do about eating, but she was busy with her work. Amal took a great bite from her half, pulling her head back to tear the bread. She didn't look afraid.

I closed my eyes before biting into mine. A second afterwards, sweetness flooded my mouth. Butter and fig jam. Another mouthful later, I was still alive, and the witch was talking.

'How's your other son these days? I forget his name.'

'Wadih.'

'Yes, yes.'

Teta snorted. 'He's flying somewhere between heaven and earth. Occasionally he lands and comes to pay us a visit.' She chuckled. 'He still has the face of an angel and the tongue of a devil.'

'How he used to make me laugh. He would sit here in my kitchen and talk till the tears ran down my face. Yes, Wadih, that was his name.'

Uncle Wadih here in her kitchen!

'Or was that my husband?' She passed her hand across her eyes. 'No, it was your son. I remember now. He used to come in his car in the summertime with watermelons in the boot and take us down to . . . to . . . that place, that place down there to have a picnic.'

Teta continued picking the mint. 'Yes, with your daughter, God rest her soul. It makes my heart hurt to think of her. Why God should take the good ones . . .'

The witch was standing at the sink with her broad back to us now, the pattern of tiny faded flowers stretched tight across it like an ironing-board cover. 'Each morning the sun rises and I blame myself. It sets and I blame myself again.'

'She was a kind girl,' murmured Teta.

'Kind?' The witch clutched a single fork with bent prongs. 'My poor child.' The cloth-wrapped head sank forwards. 'My poor, poor soul.'

When we left, Teta took me straight to church, perhaps to keep off the evil of the place, and since we were there anyway, I prayed: that Papi would get better, and that Teta wouldn't remember I hadn't apologized about the chickens. I prayed too that Naji would stop being angry all the time without saying what about, and that Mami would be happier. And Teta prayed, her eyes closed, lips moving, body rocking lightly from side to side.

Walking back, I asked, 'Where does she come from, the woman who used to be your friend?'

'From a village a long way from here, just like me.'

'Not the same village?'

'No, not the same one.'

As we passed the bakery that was only a hole in the wall, the baker scooped out a *man'oosheh* on a wooden shovel and, wrapping it in paper, handed it to a waiting boy.

'Teta, does she really know Uncle Wadih?'

'Yes. She knew him when he was a young man.'

I kicked a stone and sent it rolling into the dust. 'Why did you stop being friends?'

She gave a funny sort of a smile. 'They were too greedy, her and that husband of hers. They wanted to get hold of as much money as they could. They had plenty, but their own money wasn't enough for them, and they had to marry off their daughter to a rich man. Still,' she continued, 'God sees everything, and He sent them more than they deserved. More than anyone deserves.'

Chapter Fourteen

Teta said it always rained on Good Friday, and it did, a fine soaking rain as they carried the Christ-figure into the church on a stretcher covered with flowers. Then the school term finished early because the shelling grew worse. It started in Beirut, but quickly moved closer until the loud whistlings were overhead, followed by a moment's silence, then a shuddering bang. Mami said that the silent moment was the most terrible because you didn't know where the bomb was going to land. We weren't allowed beyond the veranda, no matter how hard we begged, and soon ran out of things to do.

'Can't I even go to Karim's?' I asked Mami.

'No.'

'To the forest, then?' The puffy green clouds of treetops were only at the bottom of the slope, but they might as well have been on the other side of the world because Mami said no.

Day by day, as spring turned to summer, the forest would be changing, its old skin peeling off like a scab to uncover a shiny new softness that was only there at this time of year. Down there, the whole place smelt as rich as a half-cooked cake. I wanted to see the rock-roses open their pink and white flowers with impossibly thin petals; to find the green and white lilies that still held the last rainwater, and hunt out the rarer ones, foul-smelling things with a single red petal wrapped round a black column. I wanted to see bees and caterpillars, squat to watch the march and scurry of ants. I wanted to be in the forest again, before it was gone.

Naji explained that Israel had invaded Lebanon, which meant that, ever since, the adults had been talking about it. Mostly it was Papi and the Rose Man, who sat perched on the sofa like a boy on a wall. Sometimes Teta was there too shelling peas or picking grit out of lentils, her half-moon glasses balanced on the end of her nose.

They argued about the invasion, about dates and places and who had done what. They talked of Begin and the plan for a Greater Israel, of American money and weapons pouring in for the Maronites who would help Israel invade. Of Bashir Jumayyil who was the people's hero, and how he hated Syria, hated the Palestinians, and on top of that was an army man, a military leader.

When the Rose Man wasn't visiting and there was no news to watch on television, the radio was the only thing Papi cared about. In the evening, he sat pointing the metal aerial first this way then that, turning the dial by a hair's width to receive the station he wanted. Slowly, his fingers felt their way to the quiet places between the sizzles, his hunched body only loosening when voices spluttered into life. Then he would set the radio back on the shelf and sit in the gloom with his nose, cheeks and forehead lit by a candle on the table. The rest of him would vanish, and the only movement would be the sparkle of his eyes catching the light as they followed Mami round the room, watched her pick up a cushion, clear the dinner-table, come in with her sewing basket. The only sound would be the voices on the radio, the thunder of bombs falling in the valley, and the click of his new string of worry beads.

I thought about asking Naji about the dust girl, but he wasn't the same Naji he used to be so I decided to ask the Rose Man instead. The Rose Man had been friends with Papi a long time. He might know what had happened.

The next time he came to our house, I waited outside the living room for his conversation with Papi to finish so I could follow him outside. The door was wide open. Teta sat working on a piece of crochet, but Papi and the Rose Man were arguing about the invasion again. Papi said it would solve the Palestinian problem. They were already naming their camps after Palestinian towns, he said, but the Rose Man didn't agree. He pointed to Papi's newspaper. 'Haven't you seen the pictures? The Israelis forcing their way along the coast, destroying towns and villages, leaving a trail of corpses?'

Like Hansel and Gretel, I thought, leaving a trail of breadcrumbs to show them the way home.

Mami had come in to clear away their coffee-cups. 'Soon they'll close the airport,' I heard her whimper as she left the room, 'and we'll be left behind.' She was right. Many of my classmates had already gone abroad with their families.

Teta's needle moved quickly, catching the thick white yarn, pulling and unhooking it. The pattern in the piece of work was full of gaps like a pretty net. The curves of it made me think of Papi's curly, beautiful handwriting again.

Shelling swelled outside, a roaring like waves, and Papi's voice rose angry above it. 'What else was Jumayyil to do? Do you forget Dammour?'

The Rose Man sucked his false teeth so his mouth looked as if it needed pumping with a plunger, then pushed them back into place. 'What the Palestinians did in Dammour, raping and cutting parts of people off – breasts, genitals – murdering women and children in front of each other, was unforgivable. But then they all do that, all of them. Ours too. It's a man who pulls the trigger, not a flag. There is no good side and bad side in this.'

'Enough. Enough of such talk,' murmured Teta.

I didn't like it either, so I wandered from room to room instead. Each room smelt different. Naji was painting toy soldiers so his room smelt of enamel paint and the old trainers he wouldn't let Mami throw away. My bedroom smelt of cotton and books, Mami and Papi's room smelt of ironed sheets. The silvery sharpness of detergent wafted from the bathroom, the dining room smelt of polish, and in the kitchen, where Mami was kneading a great ball of dough, the air was tickly warm with the scent of yeast and olive oil.

Turning the dough over, Mami's hands sank one after the other into the whiteness at a steady, comforting speed. Sweat stood out on her forehead and upper lip as she pressed down the dough. A drop fell into it and was folded in.

There was a slow drip coming from the sink too, where Mami had placed an empty plastic bottle beneath the drinking-water tap. Water didn't often come out of that tap any longer, but she left it on so that when it did she would catch all there was, even if it took a week to fill a couple of bottles.

Two days ago I'd discovered that if I stood in the hall doorway I could see every room in the flat, and I went there now. Yes, everything was still visible from here – bedrooms, kitchen, dining room, living room, bathroom – and suddenly the flat seemed small. I had never thought of it as small before. If only I could be outside.

Looking up, I pretended to stand on the ceiling. Then I was walking round the walls, stepping over the windows and round the lampshades, following the cracks toe to heel. Then I was running, running round the white walls like a spider, scuttling up the curtains, along the tops of picture frames, balancing in the corner, hurrying down to the window.

The shutters rattled as another shell landed, and there was a pause in the conversation while they waited for the sound to die away.

'History is happening faster than we can keep up,' Papi was saying. 'How many dozens of factions are there? How many changes in allegiance? How many battles and struggles, one day with this group and the next with another? But for the person who lives here time stands still.'

For a while, the faint rasp of thread being pulled by Teta's crochet needle was the only sound in the room now, and finally she spoke. 'What do I know? All I can tell you is that as far back as I remember there have been different people here. Even our food comes from different Gods: Maronites grow apples, Sunnis grow oranges and lemons, Greek Orthodox grow olives.' She unravelled some more yarn from her ball. 'Not much has changed in the last ten years. Only the children have been born and have grown, that's the only thing that's changed.'

'You watch your children go to school not knowing whether they'll come back,' said Papi. 'And down in Beirut, people walk along the streets asking themselves which of the cars parked around them might explode. "You have to go on living until you're killed." That's their motto, and now it's getting to be the same here.' He looked at the Rose Man. 'No, my friend, the sooner this sort of living is over the better, no matter if the Israelis flatten half the buildings in Beirut.'

'And the people in them, the children?' replied the Rose Man.

'It may get worse, but after that . . .' Papi took a great breath. 'Wait and see.'

When the Rose Man left, I followed him out onto the veranda.

He looked round. 'What is it, little girl?'

I didn't know how to put my question.

'Well?' he said.

'Do you remember when Papi used to go out? When he used to go to Beirut?'

'Is that all?' He took a better grip on the walking-stick. 'Yes, I remember.'

'Why did he go there?'

He frowned, looking at me curiously. 'On business. He had people to see and stock to buy. Don't you know that?'

'But something bad happened to Papi, didn't it? Please tell me. Please.'

'No.' He looked away. 'Don't ask me about her.'

'Her?' I hadn't asked about anyone. 'The girl? The girl covered in dust?' I could tell from his face that he knew.

'You know about her,' I said. I'd learnt Papi's lines by heart, like a poem:

Age: 6 to 8 years
Height: small, not yet chest-high
Hair: long and brown

136

Eyes: brown
Clothes: flip-flops and a dress, couldn't tell what colour

Then there was the nail polish where she'd sucked her thumb, and the sand and dirt all over her – *on her eyelashes, round her mouth, and in the single crease on her throat.*

'Who was she?'

The Rose Man turned away to examine his rosebushes, twisting the leaves back to check for disease. Over winter, the roses had shrivelled to mushy black bundles, but they were in bloom again now. He fingered the buds, touched one of the fully open flowers, then let it go. It bounced gently, the leaves whispering to each other. 'Don't let it bother you,' he said. 'It's nothing for you to worry about.'

'But I want to know!'

There was a screech, followed by a deep bang that made everything tremble.

When the sound died away, the Rose Man said, 'You'd better go indoors now, little girl,' and started to shuffle off.

'Wait, please!'

'I told you, you mustn't ask me,' said the Rose Man. 'It's not my business. That's something for your family to tell, not me.'

A loud crack from the valley made a bird fly chattering out of a pine tree.

'Ruba!' It was Papi calling. 'Come inside. Can't you hear the shells falling?'

When I went back into the living room, Teta was still there. I watched the pulling and twisting of her crochet needle, the complicated pattern it made from the lacy thread. Her beautiful net had grown larger.

Chapter Fifteen

The days and weeks dripped past with the water from the drinking tap and the wax from the guttering candles. The house shook and the earth shook. Mortar shells exploded, leaving shrapnel embedded deep in the walls. From above my bedroom window, Naji dug out two pieces of jagged, silver-black metal and dropped them, echoing, into his tall canister.

When it was quiet, Papi or Mami would open the shop for an hour or two, or go to the market and come back with bags of food. Naji and I grew tired of *burghul* and rice. Meat was hard to come by, and harder still to keep fresh with so little electricity, when the fridge had to be opened and shut quickly to keep the coldness inside.

On television, the newsreaders sounded panicked, and there were pictures of people strapping mattresses, carpets, chairs and tables onto the tops of cars. In Papi's newspaper, I saw a photo of a woman sitting next to a pile of rubble holding her head in both hands, her mouth open in a scream. And sticking out from between two large pieces of stone was a child's arm wearing two bangles and a ring.

When I asked Naji about it, he said the Israeli army had reached Beirut and was flattening a path right through the middle, exploding apartment blocks with people still in them to make a way for their tanks to get through. 'Like ploughing,' he said. 'It's to get the Palestinians out. Ever since they were thrown out of Jordan and came here, they've been trying to make out like Lebanon's theirs – the south, Beirut, the Beqaa valley. That's why they're always fighting with Lebanese groups.' He beamed. 'But now we've got old Israeli planes from America, and they only have Russian stuff from the Syrians.' But when I asked if that meant we were going to win, he shrugged. 'Probably.'

We weren't allowed beyond the veranda unless it was to go to Teta's, and Naji went there often. Several times he returned with shells and bullets though, and wouldn't say where he'd got them.

With nothing else to do, the days grew long, until as we stood on the veranda one afternoon, Naji announced that he was going to fly his kite by the church where the best breeze would be. Papi would be angry if he found out, I said, but when Naji opened the gate, I followed.

It was hot and still. The leaves hung from the trees like paper. A bird twittered somewhere far away, then stopped abruptly.

The church at the top of the hill road had an open veranda all the way round it. The giant wooden doors were shut, and we carried on round to the back, where the church overhung the valley that fell steeply away. From there I could see our house at the bottom of the road, and beyond, the dark treetops of the forest, fewer now than before.

'Let me have the kite,' I begged. 'You've carried it the whole way. Let me!'

'All right.'

I held the battered thing, its pale green paper creased and ripped near the edges, as though it were made of gold, while Naji gripped the tangle of string attached to it.

He pointed. 'Okay, now we'll run to the railings on the other side.' But even before he'd finished speaking, he had already started to move.

I followed at a run.

'Okay, let go! Let go!'

There was a tug on the string and the kite jerked out of my hands. For a moment the tail flapped in my face, then trailed off; the kite veered away and crashed into the wall.

'You've got to throw it higher!' snapped Naji.

'There's no breeze. That's why it didn't work.'

'Try again. And this time throw it harder, okay?'

I plodded over sullenly and picked it up. I might make my own kite, I thought. It couldn't be that difficult, and Karim would help.

'Ready?' called Naji. 'Okay, now! *Yalla!* Run!'

And I did.

'Throw it! Let it go!' he shouted.

I hurled the pasted wood and paper up into the air, the sun glaring in my eyes. But as I ran, the tail caught under my foot and, with a rip, the end tore off beneath my shoe.

That was when the shout came. 'Hey, Naji!'

The green-eyed gun-boy and his spotty friend were standing in the road eating *shawarma*.

'What are you doing?' called the spotty one, a trickle of sweat zigzagging down his temple.

'Nothing,' answered Naji. 'Nothing.'

The green-eyed one picked a piece of meat from his teeth.

'Want to see if we can get some more stuff from those soldiers? Maybe we can get grenade pins this time.'

'Yes,' said the other, 'and we can find out what's going on from people who know about it.'

I stepped forward to join Naji.

'Oh, that baby sister of his is here,' jeered the spotty one. 'Are you going to cry again?'

'I didn't cry!'

The gun-boy swallowed the rest of his *shawarma*, scrunched up the paper wrapping and threw it to the ground. Wiping his hands on his trousers, he said, 'Let's go and do some target practice. Coming, Naji?'

The kite lay between me and Naji on the speckled tiles of the church veranda.

'No.' Naji sounded sorry. 'I can't today.'

Gun-boy grinned. 'Come on,' he said to his friend. 'He's got to babysit.'

Above us, the sun fell on the coloured-glass saints, but they didn't glow. Looking at them from the inside they would be blooming in brilliant colours, but out here they were dull and dark.

Naji was chewing his lips as he looked after the two boys.

'You lied!' I exploded. 'You said you wouldn't play with them any more and you did!' My face felt hot.

'I didn't play with them. We don't *play*. We talk and . . .' his shoulders rose and fell in a shrug '. . . we learn stuff.'

'You promised!' Anger filled me up, reached my ears and eyes, came out hot from my nostrils.

Naji began to reel in the kite.

'All those times you said you were going to Teta's you were with them! You lied the whole time!'

Naji seemed uncomfortable. The kite dangled motionless from his hand, a few centimetres off the ground. Then it started to swing. It swung backwards and forwards, and all at once it rose into the air. The string in Naji's hand grew taut, the kite swooped up and, flapping its shortened tail, rushed off to the left, a green diamond against the blue sky. A wind had sprung up out of the earth.

Startled, Naji yanked at the string, but the kite pulled left and right in sharp movements, like a paper bird. Then it was the earth that was moving – moving upwards; and as it did there came a black roar, slice, roar, slice.

I screamed. With a downward swoop, the kite crashed into the church wall and fell to the ground, but Naji didn't care. He was staring wide-eyed down the hill road.

It came slowly up the middle of our street, not touching the ground but floating a little way above it, a black metal giant, roaring the whole time, never stopping for breath.

I stumbled towards Naji and hid behind him. 'What is it?'

He twisted himself out of my grasp. 'You're hurting my arm!' But he didn't take his eyes off it.

I took hold of him again, and this time he didn't shake me off.

'It's a helicopter! A gunship helicopter!' Still clutching the kite-string in one hand, he pointed as though I couldn't see it for myself. 'Look! It's using the buildings and trees as cover so the militia in the valley on the other side of the hill won't be able to see it and shoot it down.'

I cried out, but my voice was whisked away by the rising wind and noise.

Balanced in mid-air, the thing slid up the hill until it reached the top of the road. It stopped below the church veranda, then rose. First the rotating metal flower, then the ugly bulb hanging underneath, straight up before us. From where he stood in front of me against the railings, Naji could have reached out and touched it.

Dust swirled in the road below, and the thunder of the blades filled every tiny space in the world. It throbbed through my bones and crowded into my head. My hair fluttered like tissue paper held out of a car window. I gripped Naji and Naji gripped the railing, while behind us, the kite chattered and flapped against the wall. Even the church seemed to be leaning away.

The helicopter hung there, a giant metal ball, as all around us the world waved and rippled. Spiky things poked out of the front and sides of the machine, and the sun glinted off it in spears of light. Apart from the big propeller at the top, there was a smaller one on the green tail next to some printed white numbers.

Then suddenly it changed, or the way I was seeing it changed. Because now I was looking at two round glass eyes, and it was an enormous bee with a dozen stings and sharp, whirry metal wings. Yes, a giant bee, that's what it was. But as something moved inside the bee's eyes, it became a helicopter again. The spiky things at the front became guns, those at the sides missiles, and the fleck in one eye became a man.

The man in the helicopter was wearing a uniform, and sitting right behind him was another man. Both had helmets on. The one in front and lower down was young, the other older with a thin moustache. Then the young one pointed at Naji and me with his mouth moving fast.

They'd caught us. We'd been caught flying a kite on the church veranda where we shouldn't have been. Perhaps someone had told them we were there, and now they were going to swivel those long side-guns round to point straight at us, one for me and one for Naji, and shoot us dead. And I would suddenly be under the rubble like the girl in the newspaper.

I wanted to tell them it wasn't our fault. I looked at the closest one – maybe he would understand – but he was looking somewhere else now, and when he glanced back at us, his eyes were sad.

Naji twirled round, and on the other side of the main road, the nut-shop owner stood in his doorway. He was shouting, but no words reached us through the noise. He started to make funny movements, shooing us away, and above him, gaping at the window with his large hands wrapped round the bars, was Ali.

Then we were racing down the veranda steps, running round the corner and down the hill.

'Hurry!' shouted Naji.

There was sand in my mouth. Wind whirled round my head, blowing the thoughts about in my brain. We weren't halfway down the hill when an enormous blast came from behind us. At the same time a pebble rolled under my foot and I fell. In front of me, Naji stopped and turned but he wasn't looking at me. He was pointing back.

'They're shooting the missiles!'

It was Papi who gripped us, first one then the other, by the shoulders, as Mami sank into a chair. I felt small and transparent. Up there on the church veranda, I'd thought Teta's fears about someone dying were coming true. Then there was the sound of a sharp smack, and when I looked round, Naji was holding his cheek.

'Didn't I tell you not to step outside the veranda? Didn't I?' I had never seen Papi so angry. The whirring and shooting outside fitted his mood. 'You could have got yourself and your sister killed!'

Naji's hand was still over his cheek. He was glaring at Papi.

'Go to your room. Now!'

When Naji was gone, it was me who answered Papi's questions. I told them about the helicopter and the two men and the missiles and the way everything had been filled with noise.

'They're Israelis firing back across the valley,' Papi explained to Mami as the noise from outside faded away.

'Back at who?' asked Mami.

'The Druze, probably.'

'But I thought they were Israel's ally,' said Mami.

'Things change day by day in this war. Now they're being shelled by them. There are militia hiding in the forests all around this area, and when they shoot at us, the Israelis shoot back.'

But that wasn't the end of the questions I had to answer, and before long everything that had happened was out. I had told Papi and Mami about the older boys. I had given Naji away.

Papi's voice was dangerously quiet. 'Go and fetch your brother.'

I did as I was told, but couldn't bring myself to tell Naji why he was wanted. By the time we'd come back out, Mami was ironing, and Papi was no longer in his chair, but facing her across her scarred ironing-board.

'I won't allow it, Aida, do you hear? I won't allow my son to hang around with butcher-boys.'

Mami's ironing-board creaked as she pressed her iron into the corners of a pair of pants, folded them and pressed down again. A cloud of steam rose and vanished in front of Papi's face.

As I went to the sofa and hurriedly picked up a book about Ali Baba, Naji threw me a look that made it clear I was his enemy now.

A tea-towel replaced the pants on the ironing-board, and the creaking began again. The pointy iron searched into the edges and hems of the worn cloth, back and forth, but Mami's mouth was a sealed line.

Papi swung round. 'Where did those boys take you? Up to see their soldier friends?' The spilt vinegar mark on his forehead was clear and dark. 'Did you feel at home there? What did they teach you, *ha*?' He waited, while beside him more steam rose. 'Are you enjoying it? Tell me, are you having fun being with such . . . such . . .' The words ran out.

Naji set his jaw. 'I'll do what I want. The other boys' parents don't—'

'Other boys' parents,' exploded Papi, 'are either too stupid or too heartless to care what their children do.' A hand rose to his head and his voice dropped. 'Everyone in this country's going mad, mad with the taste of blood.'

Hee-haw, hee-haw. Mami was ironing socks now.

'I wasn't with them.'

A fist banged down on the table. 'Don't lie to me!'

'Nabeel, please,' said Mami.

'Don't interfere in this, Aida.' Papi leant heavily on the dining-room table and glared across it at Naji. 'I know. I've heard, so don't lie to me.'

I dodged Naji's eyes behind my book. All around, anger and steam floated hot in the thick air.

'My son isn't going to become one of those dogs.' Papi's face was colourless, a lump of sandstone someone had scraped at to make a mouth, nose and eyes.

Naji was breathing fast. 'I don't want to be your son. I'm *not* your son!'

'Do you hear how my own son's talking to me?' said Papi.

'I told you, I'm not your son! I don't care if I do look like you! And you're not my father.' Naji was trembling all over. 'You're – you're nothing!'

The ironing-board stopped creaking. Papi seemed to grow larger. He leant across the table on outspread hands. 'What did you say?'

The words flowed out of Naji now. 'I said you're nothing! You can't tell me what to do. You can't tell me anything! You can't tell me who I can talk to or be friends with or where I can go. Because you haven't done anything for me in years!'

I held the colourful picture of turbaned thieves between me and the anger in the room. A smell of burning spread out as, with a jolt, Mami lifted her iron off the board.

Papi's hands left the table. He walked round it, straight up to Naji. A hand gripped Naji's shoulder, making him hunch with pain. I thought about racing over to save him but couldn't move.

A burnt sock hung from Mami's hand.

'You dare to talk to me like that?' said Papi through his teeth. 'Who keeps this roof over your head and food in your mouth?'

Naji looked small but his voice was strong. 'Mami and Teta are the ones who work and cook. You don't even do as much as them, as much as women! Because you're a coward.'

Papi's free hand flew up to hit Naji. But then it dropped. 'Aida, I don't want him to have anything to do with those boys.' He was looking at Naji but talking to Mami, his voice splitting and cracking like chips of rock. 'Do you hear me?'

'You're not a father.' Naji's words tripped over themselves. 'Fathers do things. They walk and talk and look neat and smell nice. They know things and buy you ice-cream and make you laugh. They have a job and treat you like a man.'

I heard the breath leak out of Papi, and Naji grimaced in pain as Papi's fingers dug into him. Then Papi's arm fell to his side. He wilted like the thirsty cactus outside. 'Go to your room.'

Naji's face was cold. 'I hate you. They all hate you.' He turned away. A moment later his bedroom door banged shut, and guilt pooled inside me, dark as oil.

Chapter Sixteen

That evening there was a strange stillness in the house. When I crept to the door of Naji's room, no sound came from inside. The electricity was cut so there was no television, only the crackle of Papi's radio. He held it close to his ear and it whispered terrible things to him, things that made him look scared and bite his lip till it bled.

In the kitchen, Mami was cooking as though she were in a race, stirring furiously with her wooden spoon and gazing into the bottom of the pot as if she wanted to be there. Later, when she came in to draw the curtains, she stood listening to the radio and winding her apron string round her finger.

'Get him to come up, for mercy's sake. He'll get killed if he stays down there,' she said finally.

Papi pulled himself up and went to the phone. For the next half an hour there was nothing but the sound of stirring from the kitchen and dialling from the dining room. I drew a picture of *Scotlanda* with Missizbel in it, surrounded by trees, butterflies and three smiling children, me, Karim and Amal, while Papi's finger swept round the plastic dial again and again, always selecting the same set of numbers.

I jumped when he finally spoke. 'Wadih? Can you hear me?' Papi bent over the receiver. '*Yalla*, my brother, come up to Ein Douwra. What are you waiting for? Just get in your car and drive.'

There was a short silence.

'But they're murdering people down there, using their flats as bases, no matter if you're a Christian or not.'

I sharpened a red pencil to colour in the children's smiles.

'What's it to you if the airport's closed?' asked Papi. 'Why? What's in Switzerland?' He listened. 'What work? Your company's been closed for a month now.'

Mami came to stand in the doorway.

'Don't be foolish, Wadih. Hello, hello? Can you hear me?'

Slowly, he replaced the receiver. 'The line went dead,' he told Mami.

'What did he say?' she asked.

'That he had work. What kind of work is there when people are either walled up in their houses or fleeing for their lives?'

'Didn't you ask him?'

'He said he'd be all right.' Papi pushed his fingers through his hair. 'He's crazy! Who stays in Beirut at a time like this if they have somewhere else to go? He said . . . he said he had contacts.'

'What contacts?'

But Papi shook his head. 'I don't know.'

Naji's door was ajar so I pushed it open. He was sitting on his bed whittling a piece of wood with a penknife, and didn't even look up.

150

'Uncle Wadih was going to come up, but now he's not,' I announced, knowing how excited he always got about any news of Uncle Wadih.

But he simply carried on whittling.

'Papi can't understand why he stays in Beirut because it's so dangerous now.'

Still no reaction, just the steady scrape-scrape-scrape of the penknife against the wood.

'He said something about Uncle having contacts. What's contacts?' I asked, but there was no reply.

I watched the growing pile of flakes at his feet. Soon the piece of wood was nothing but a pile of sawdust. Naji got up, dusted himself and put his cassette-player on. He turned it up loud, so I left.

When the electricity flicked on that evening, he came out to sit cross-legged on the floor and watch television, but never once looked at Papi or at me.

'Did you see how he fell over?' I laughed once, pointing at the screen, and he swivelled round with friendly eyes, then caught himself.

But there weren't many funny things on television. When the news came on, the men in suits were worried, the camera lights glinting on their sweaty faces. Then came pictures of rubble and guns, the twisted metal of exploded cars, buildings shot through until there were more holes than stone; pictures of crying children, crying men and women, and clouds of dust from the carved-up earth.

I didn't think Naji's silence would last, but he was good at it. The next morning I followed him onto the veranda and hung on the railings watching the planes fighting in the sky above us. They sped up like rockets then fell, left and right and up and down, shooting missiles at each other.

'It's always those two types,' I said, 'the big fat ones that go fast, and those thinner ones. It's not really fair.'

Drumming his fingers on the railings, Naji ignored me and carried on watching, his head tilted back.

'Look!' I pointed. To the left above the treetops, a plane burst into bright yellow flames and left a black trail as it dropped. 'A skinny one again.' We'd seen three get hit in the last week.

My finger followed the plane's path, then the parachute that drifted down from it. A short while afterwards came the hum of a truck engine that grew loud, then faded away.

'What's that?' I asked, but there was no answer. A little later, another thin plane was blasted sideways out of its path. When I opened my eyes again, I saw that it had snapped in two, and the front half was dangling like a broken toy. 'It's always those skinny ones that get shot,' I whispered, waiting for the parachute. But none came out of that plane.

'Mami,' called Naji into the kitchen, 'come and see the fighter planes.'

She came out wiping the suds from her arms.

'See those ones?' said Naji. 'Those big ones? They're F-15s and F-16s – Israeli planes. And the other thin ones, like that one over there with the black nose, they're the Syrian planes. That one's a MiG-21. And that one's a MiG-23. They're older and slower.'

She watched until a fat plane roared past lower than the others. 'Inside,' she said, herding us to the door. 'Haven't you had enough of war?'

'Can I go down the road to watch some more?' asked Naji.

'After yesterday?'

'I won't go far.'

'No.'

'I wanted to see another parachute,' I said as we went into the living room. 'We saw one fall just now, and afterwards there was a noise of a truck.'

Papi grunted. 'Jeeps. They send out jeeps to round up the men who fall from those planes.'

Naji's mouth opened to say something, then shut again with a *tac* of teeth.

'You mean they rescue them?' I said.

'Rescue.' Papi stared at the carpet. 'Maybe they'll hold them in exchange for something, maybe they'll torture them. Or maybe they'll just kill them outright.'

From the minute I told on him, Naji stopped speaking to me. There were no more jokes, no more laughing at me when I was silly, and no more explaining how things worked. He didn't even shout at me to go away or leave him alone, just pretended I wasn't there. He stopped speaking to Papi too.

'I only told Papi the truth,' I told him more than once, but it made no difference. To him I didn't exist.

'Why is it so quiet in here?' Karim whispered when he came round one morning two weeks later. 'Is someone sick?'

'No, just nobody's talking to anybody else,' I explained. 'But how come you're here?' Karim hadn't stepped inside the house since Eid el Burbara.

He sat down on the bed. 'I'm leaving. We're going to Abu Dhabi.'

'What?'

'Tomorrow.'

'Tomorrow! Are you sure?'

'I told you my father was trying to arrange it.'

'But I didn't think . . .' I had a sinking feeling in my stomach. 'Are you really going?'

He nodded, but didn't look happy about it as he should have.

'Where's Abu Dhabi?'

'I don't know.'

Naji would know, but it was useless to ask him. 'If you come round tonight, we can go out and watch the red streaks in the sky where bombs are flying in the valley. Sometimes you can see the flash when they land.'

But he shook his head. 'I can't. We have to finish packing.'

Around him, the diamond pattern on the bedspread turned into a hundred sharp, separate islands.

'Will you ever come back?'

He burst out into a laugh. 'Of course I'm coming back! I'm leaving most of my things here. I'll come back next year when the war's over, sooner if it finishes quickly.' Then his smile died away.

'Don't you want to go?'

'Not really. I don't know anyone in Abu Dhabi.'

As he got up, I took in his brown knees, the hole in his right sock, the sticking-out ears, the wide mouth, the hair that looked as though it had been burnt into a frizz.

'Karim.'

'Yes?'

'It'll be like going to the moon.'

We stared at each other for a moment, then he bent to tie his shoelace.

'I'm going now,' he said when he straightened up again. 'I'll come over when I get back.'

'Okay.'

''Bye,' he said.

''Bye.'

My chest felt hollow, and after Karim left, there was a new emptiness about each room that hadn't been there before, so I went to the only other place Mami would allow me to go.

Teta was kneeling on a folded cloth on her kitchen floor. A giant stone bowl stood in front of her full of *zaatar* that she was pounding with a large pestle.

I sat down on the wooden stool beside the stove. The smell of the thyme filled the room, thick as a forest, while the thud of stone on stone travelled across the floor and through my fingertips like the beating of an enormous heart. I watched the shudder of hanging flesh on Teta's upper arms, memorized the rotating grind of the pestle against the herb, felt the tremble of the great stone heart with each thump.

When she paused to wipe her sleeve across her forehead, I spoke: 'Teta, Karim's leaving.'

'Many people are going. Anyone who can is getting out.'

The wrinkled skin of her chest showed as she unbuttoned the top of her shirt to let in the cool air, and I saw the little wad of tissues she always kept tucked in her shoulder strap for when she cried.

'Teta, is Naji going to become like Papi?'

The grey pestle lay at an angle. 'Naji?'

'Yes. Will he become . . . you know, like Papi?' I didn't know the proper words to describe it.

Gazing thoughtfully into the stone basin, Teta breathed the green smell deep into her body. 'No, he won't become like your father.'

'But he's different now. He doesn't play so much and he's stopped talking to me.'

'Don't mind him. He's still your brother.' She rolled her sleeves up further.

'Papi said that the children's judge hanged himself. What does that mean?'

Teta adjusted the cloth beneath her knees. 'When did he say that?'

'When he found out Naji was playing with those older boys. Who made the judge hang himself, Teta? Was it our fault?'

She smiled. 'No, *habibti*, it's not real. It just means that nobody can understand the mind of a child or why they do the things they do, not even a children's judge.'

The pounding started again, and I leant against the shivering metal side of the oven until the shiver was moving inside my chest. The crunch of thyme was broken occasionally when the pestle caught the stone bowl directly with a loud *clack*.

'But what if Naji does become like Papi? What then?'

The grinding continued as Teta pushed with her hands, her elbows, her shoulders and body, leaning into the basin and back again faster than before, forwards and backwards, heavy body pushing heavy stone.

'I don't want him to get that way!'

The pounding stopped and Teta's shoulders relaxed. She laid down the pestle. 'Don't be afraid. Your father, that was different. He changed nearly overnight. It was different.'

'But why?' I hesitated before asking the question that no one ever asked. 'Why did he change?'

Teta took up some of the thick green-brown powder and rubbed it between her thumb and fingers, letting it fall into the stone bowl again. 'Some things change and you can't change them back again,' she said.

'But Teta, what happened to make him like that?'

She scooped up more *zaatar*, rubbed it between her fingers and let it sift out again. A spatter of sweat lay across her forehead, and the tingling smell of the mountains rose from the bowl, filling every corner of the kitchen.

'It's because of the girl, isn't it?'

Her eyelids sprang up. 'Girl?'

'I spoke to the Rose Man about it, and he wouldn't tell me, but I know it's because of something that happened, something to do with a girl. Please tell me, Teta. *You*'ll tell me, won't you?'

For a long time Teta stared into her bowl. When she finally spoke, her voice was deep and scratchy. 'That day he went to Beirut . . . You do a good turn for a friend and look what happens. You visit a sick man and the world changes.'

Would she tell me?

Teta didn't look up. Her hands were still now. They lay curved over the lip of the basin. 'He was in an area of Beirut where it was dangerous to be at that time. He had just visited a sick friend of his, a man he did business with for the shop, and a child comes up to him, a little girl carrying a bottle. And in the bottle is an ear, a pickled ear.'

The smell of thyme stuck to my skin and slipped into my hair.

'"Here," said the girl, pushing it at him. "Buy it. Take it. It only costs a little."' The lines gathered round Teta's eyes. 'They cut pieces off the people they killed and gave them to the children to sell. You could buy someone's finger or nose or ear, a woman's, a man's, maybe one that had belonged to your friend.'

157

I felt sick as I saw Mami's ears pink as shells, Naji's small and neat, Karim's like handles. And the smell of the *zaatar*, sharp as splinters, filled my head.

'What was God thinking?' Teta asked. 'A little girl, dirty and barefoot, pushing the bottle at your father in some Beirut alleyway. And what was he to do? What would anyone have done? He shouts at her, tells her to get away from him, to take that thing away, but she won't. "Where are you going?" she calls. "Let me walk with you a little way." He shouts at her again to go away but she says she has nowhere to go. "You don't have to buy it, Mister. Just let me walk with you, that's all." Probably she didn't want to go home – if you can call those refugee slums a home.'

I gripped the sides of my stool with both hands to steady my thoughts. The frayed rope felt rough, its broken fibres sticking out like thick hairs.

'But your father won't accept. Such a sight, such a thing for a child to be clutching to her belly. He doesn't want it near him. So he shouts at her some more, worse this time, trying to scare her away, and in the end she understands. She backs away from him out of the alleyway and into the open. And then she falls. The bottle smashes and she falls among the glass. She doesn't get up again.' Teta swallowed hard. 'Who can blame him if his eyes can't forget it?'

Her hands remained slung over the grey edge of the basin. They would never move again; they would stay there, curled round the mortar for ever.

'Your father looked up and a gunman was leaning out of a church window high up. A Palestinian, God shorten his days. He was wearing one of those plastic children's masks, and when he lifted it up he was laughing. "Your girl?" he called. "Your child?"'

The dewdrops of water on Teta's forehead had blended together.

'That was what your father told us. It came out of his mouth fast that day, and he wrote down those things about the girl. "So I can find out who she was," he said, "so I won't forget what she looked like."' Teta closed her eyes. 'As if he could forget. He tried to find out who she was: he asked the authorities in Beirut, visited that spot again and again, knocked on every door he saw, but he couldn't find out. Such deaths get lost. In this country such deaths are nothing.' She opened her eyes again. '"It was my fault," he said, "all my fault," and no one could tell him otherwise. "I shouldn't have shouted at her," he said, "I shouldn't have told her to go away." *Ach*,' moaned Teta, 'what was God thinking? What was He thinking?'

Mami bent to look at me as I took a seat at the lunch table. 'Are you sick?' she asked, but I shook my head.

I rolled the stuffed vineleaves round my plate, and the shiny green fingers left streaks of oily juice. Pickled fingers. Pickled noses and ears. I glanced up at Papi. He seemed different – broken, as though someone had let him fall from a height. He had shouted at a little girl and watched her get killed. A man in a mask had done it. The man had laughed. Laughed. And at Papi's feet, broken glass, a dead girl, an ear.

There was no sound in the room except for the clink of ice in Papi's glass of *arak*, the tearing of bread, the chewing of food, the scrape of Mami's fork, and the ticking of the gold-rimmed clock on the wall behind her. The smell of chickpeas and potatoes made me feel ill.

'Aren't you hungry, Ruba?' Mami asked.

Naji still wouldn't look at me, but today I didn't care. He was smiling to himself. 'Shall I tell you a joke, Mami? When God was creating the world, He said, "Today I'm going to create Lebanon. It will be a country by the sea, but it'll also have snowy mountains, beautiful lakes and forests, and a thousand different kinds of flower. Fruits and vegetables will grow there, there'll be rivers and springs, and the people will have everything they need."

'When he heard all this, the angel standing next to God was confused. "But aren't You giving them too much? How will they know how to be humble if they have everything?"

'Then God started to laugh. "Everything?" He couldn't stop laughing. "Just wait and see the neighbours I'm going to give them!"'

Naji rocked with laughter and Mami smiled, but Papi didn't find it funny.

'It's a joke, Nabeel,' said Mami, 'only a joke. What else is there for him to do when he's not allowed out?'

'The rest of us manage.'

Mami took a sip of water and set the glass down again. 'We don't manage. Out there, there's nothing but the screech of crickets and the blazing sun and the empty blue sky. Every day it's the same, like living in a burning blue box without a single crack in it.'

The walls looked whiter suddenly, and the red second hand on the clock was speeding round: *tic*, tremble, *tac*, tremble, *tic*, tremble, *tac*, tremble. I thought about how one instant had changed Papi. How as he stood there in Beirut he had become a different man. As a girl fell. As a fly went past his ear, *zzzzzzt*.

160

'The children can sacrifice a little for the time being,' said Papi.

Mami slapped the table. Her voice flew across it like a shrill bird: 'Haven't we all sacrificed enough? The life we could have led . . .'

Papi breathed deeply. 'You made your decisions!'

Mami's fork slipped and scraped the plate.

'What do you think, Aida? Did you make the wrong choice?'

Mami stared as if a bomb had just fallen on the table. What had Papi said? What wrong choice was he talking about? I didn't understand.

I speared one of the glossy vineleaf fingers on my plate, leaving four tiny square holes in it. Or were they square? I wasn't sure of anything any longer. It was all breaking up into crumbs: pieces of bread that lay scattered on the table. Specks of dust that had once been a girl.

It was in the middle of the afternoon, when Mami was hanging the washing outside, that the first drop fell. There was no sound but the creak and moan of the line, and sitting on the doorstep, I saw a dark spot appear on the tile near her foot, then another. At first I thought she was crying. Then, like a rash, the ground grew spotted with small frilly-edged circles.

Mami stood clutching the bundled-up sheets in her arms, but she didn't move. She held out her hand and peered into it.

'Aren't you coming in?' I called.

Her head dipped backwards, its coiled snail of hair clinging tight, as Mami gazed up. The rain was falling in large drops now.

'But it's summer.' She looked at me, her eyes puckered against the wet. 'It never rains in summer.'

But it was raining. The world had cracked open.

Chapter Seventeen

I couldn't tell Naji what Teta had told me. The silence between us had thickened like rice pudding, and words could no longer cut through it. Even if I spoke, I wasn't certain whether he'd hear me.

Two weeks after I found out what had happened to Papi, on a searingly hot day at the end of August, shouting and hooting, banging and music came from the main street in town. Radios played through loudspeakers, and the news blared out. Across the way, a man came onto the balcony in pyjama bottoms and a white vest, still chewing his breakfast. He was holding a pistol. Hoisting his pyjama trousers a little further up his fat belly and swallowing his mouthful, he raised the pistol and fired it three times into the air. Then he turned round and went back inside to finish his meal.

Naji had climbed onto the dresser in his bedroom to watch out of the window that faced up the hill towards the main street. As I passed I saw him squirming restlessly, one foot tapping against the wood.

I found Mami and Papi talking on the veranda in front of the Rose Man's roses. Papi's voice was fast and excited, and he stood up straighter than usual.

'What's happening up there?' I interrupted.

'It's an election,' said Mami, adjusting my collar.

'An election?' Papi sounded surprised. 'It's more than that. Bashir Jumayyil, the leader of the Phalange Party, has won. He's elected to become president.'

'Is that good?' I asked. Because Papi looked happy. He sounded happy too.

'It means the war will be won and finished before long,' he replied, with a smile.

'Go in and eat your breakfast,' said Mami. 'There are *mana'eesh* inside. Papi bought them especially.'

But I refused. 'No. I don't like *zaatar* any more.'

'Not like it? Why not?'

I shrugged. 'I just don't. I'm never going to eat it again.'

Mami sighed and shook her head.

There was more hooting from up the hill. 'Can I go up there?'

'No. You stay at home with us.'

I went back to my room, kicking the edges of the rug along the way. Karim had left, and the parents of my other friends nearby watched over them like spies.

Naji's bedroom door was closed.

Picking up a yellow pencil, I hopped round the room, tapping each piece of furniture three times as I passed. The snap of firecrackers, the blare of music and the cheering of men floated about outside.

Naji had to be doing something more interesting than I was. I crept to his door and listened. 'Naji?'

He couldn't hear me. He'd pretended I didn't exist for so long now that he couldn't hear me. If I went in maybe he wouldn't see me.

'Naji?'

Still nothing.

I turned the handle and pushed open the door. There was the bed, there were the shelves and small table, and the half-open wardrobe. I checked behind the bedroom door, then I opened the wardrobe wide. But he wasn't there.

I searched the house room by room, crouching to look under tables and peering behind doors. He couldn't have gone out. I would have seen him from my bedroom or from the veranda if he had.

'What have you lost?' asked Papi as he spread open his newspaper.

'Nothing.'

Then I knew. I knew where he was and how he'd gone. If I told Papi he would explode with an angry bang. If I told Mami, it would be worse because then she'd have to tell Papi herself. And if I did either, Naji would never speak to me ever again.

For a long time I stood undecided in his room. Then I pulled open his dresser drawers and climbed up them. I swung myself over the windowsill, slipped down against the rough outer wall and dropped to the ground. Not stopping to rub my knees better, I ran panting up the hill. I didn't even stop when a stitch stabbed me in the ribs. If Naji could go, I wanted to as well.

At the top of the hill, the junction was jammed with cars and noise. I looked left and right. A haze rose from the earth, and wobbly edged cars lined the street – cars parked at angles or jutting out into the road; cars crawling slowly down its centre, hooting, with men sitting on their window-frames or sticking up out of their sunroofs clutching radios and guns, making the victory sign, shouting, chanting.

The national anthem throbbed out of one radio, a woman's singing out of another. Guns fired into the air, and along the sides of the road, people of all ages stood and watched. Taxi drivers leant against their cars, and old couples looked down from balconies and terraces.

I pushed past some people standing at the corner: a smelly, sweating man, a young woman, an excited group of boy-men. It was difficult to see through all the bodies and legs. One hand I passed held a pistol, another a rolled-up newspaper, a third a bar of chocolate. Gunshots cracked from the opposite side of the road. Someone pushed by and stood in front of me. I struggled between two bodies, threaded my way along the road, was pushed aside, stepped on someone's foot. A machine-gun held by a smiling young man rattled its fire from the top of a car, the empty cartridges tinkling onto the metal roof.

The noise was difficult to see through: the loud shots, the cheering and shouts, the music and the giant voices of newsreaders, the squeaking of tyres and hooting of horns. It mixed with the heat to fill the air so thickly that seeing came in little pieces. A tattered shoe, a banner, the scratched side of a car, a cat on top of a high wall, the wheelchair man sitting near the rubbish barrels, the cone-berries of a cypress tree beside a stone wall. And people – hot faces, smiling faces, moist hands, a child's jumping feet, rolled up shirtsleeves dark with sweat, the hem of a skirt, a flash of gold in some-one's mouth.

I looked round again. Four men were climbing onto crates carrying a cloth banner, a wave of red that fell curling onto a car beside a scooter beside a boy. A boy trying to see past two moustached men. A boy with Naji's face.

165

I ran across the street. A car braked. The noise thickened like fog, but by the time I'd reached the two men, Naji was gone. One of the men ruffled my hair as I passed, but to the left, Naji's back was moving quickly away.

'Naji!' I ran after him, pushing at bodies, avoiding a car door that opened in front of me.

Finally my hand reached out and touched his shoulder. Naji swung round, and when he saw me he breathed in sharply.

'I found you,' I said, but neither of us could hear me now.

He started walking away.

'But I found you! I knew you'd be here.' I pulled at his T-shirt and was shaken off. 'Where are you going? You're going the wrong way!'

He was heading up a steep path near the patch of scrub where we'd collected snails. Half scrambling, he stepped over a low wall on the right and went in among the trees.

'Are you going to look for more shells?' I called, panting to keep up, the heat stinging my eyes.

But he wasn't searching. He was peering between the tree-trunks to find a good view of the road below. I went after him, glancing down at the crush of cars and the tops of heads. It was no cooler up here. If anything it was even hotter, the trapped heat of a sealed pot boiling over a fire.

'Can you see well from there?'

It was a little quieter among the trees, which seemed to spread a silence of their own. Below us a line of cars moved from left to right, another line from right to left. Voices swirled, banners waved, victory signs stabbed upwards into the air.

It was a finger of noise that found us, only a little sound, a singing whistle followed by a *thup*.

To my left, Naji was squatting, craning this way and that to see what was going on. Down on the road, a group of cars playing extra loud music was passing. The black spikes of rifles and lumpier branches of machine-guns poked out of the windows and sunroofs. Bullets cracked through the air.

There was another whistle, closer by, and another *thup*. I saw the hole in the tree in front of me this time.

'Naji! Come and see! It made a hole!'

But he stayed where he was, so I hurried over and crouched beside him. The soil felt cooked and warm. For a moment he seemed annoyed, even though he didn't look at me.

In the road, young men dressed in green with big gold crosses round their necks were chanting an angry chant. One raised a rifle and fired into the sky. At the side of the road, a pistol floated up, aimed over people's heads, and snapped.

Now Naji heard it too: bullets zinging among the trees like wasps, the *thup*s as they hit the trees.

Away to the right, a machine-gun clicked fast as a sewing-machine.

Standing up, Naji swivelled this way and that, following the whistles, peering round at the tree-trunks to find the holes.

'Come away, Naji.'

Another bullet buzzed past: *thup*.

Wide-eyed, Naji swung round to see.

'I want to go home now!' I said. 'Take me home.'

Something sped past my ear, and I waited for the sound of it hitting wood. There should have been a *thup* but there was none. Instead Naji squealed and fell over next to me.

'Naji?' He was lying curled up, not moving. 'Naji, get up! *Yalla!*'

I put out a hand to shake him, then stopped. A dark pool was forming in the earth.

I tried to say his name and couldn't. I touched him lightly on the shoulder, but he didn't move.

I grabbed a man's hand and pulled. 'My brother!' I yelled in his ear. 'They've shot him! Up there! They've shot him and now he's dead!'

I ran crying and stumbling down the hill behind them, my cheeks burning, and with a ringing in my ears. I couldn't see, hear or speak. Everything was glued up, everything except the tears that wouldn't stop coming.

They took Naji, carried him away from me as Mami wailed like an injured dog, and I was left alone with Teta.

'It's your fault!' I shouted, burying my face in her and breathing in lavender and garlic. 'You *said* someone would die. You said it, and now . . .'

I couldn't cry. But sitting on her bed, Teta beat her chest and cried for us both. She prayed to the Virgin Mary. She rocked and moaned and wiped her eyes, dragging at the wrinkled skin, and pressed my head closer into her chest.

There were streaks of blood on my clothes, Naji's blood, but I wouldn't let her take them off me.

I wandered, searching, from room to room. The heat had suddenly poured out of the day. Afternoon had turned to evening and Teta's flat was dim and cool, a strange place for my throbbing head, churning with pictures and words that wouldn't settle. I walked round Teta's flat yet it wasn't hers that I saw but ours again, ours filled with silent spaces. In my mind, I walked from Mami's kitchen where a plate lay smashed on the floor, through the living room with its empty chair, into my bedroom with the yellow pencil and the book I'd read too many times thrown down on the floor. Finally I stood in the doorway of Naji's room. It was the same as I remembered but something was wrong, as though a wall were missing or a door hadn't been shut. Or as if someone was hiding, as if Naji himself was crouching in the wardrobe, squashed between his schoolbag and his smelly trainers, holding in his laughter while he waited for the right moment. Then he'd jump out with a great yell and drag me, laughing, to the floor. 'You believed it!' he'd cry, the tears squeezing out of his eyes. 'You believed it all: that I'd never speak to you again – *me* not speak to *you*! – and that they shot me dead.' He would barely be able to breathe for laughing. And I'd laugh too and be embarrassed, and at the same time feel a rush of happiness with the world for making Naji my brother.

But I was in Teta's bedroom, staring down through the window at the valley, a grey carpet of pine trees under a grey evening sky. Nothing had colour any more. The life had drained from everything in dark pools hours ago. In that tiny moment, a *thup* had stopped him, just as it had stopped Papi, and now the floors and flowers and books and trees didn't want to go on. And I knew that if I put out a hand and touched the wall, it would give like a soft balloon a week after the party.

As I turned away from the window, *she* was in front of me on Teta's dressing-table. The Virgin Mary. That little little woman in her blue dress, with both arms outstretched and a pink plastic smile on her plastic face.

Picking her up, I bit down hard. I bit down on her feet and hands. I bit down on her face. I bit down on her golden

169

crown until it began to turn between my teeth. And when it did, I unscrewed it and drank the holy water from her head, every last drop. Then, wiping my mouth, I left her lying crownless and empty on the dressing-table.

The corridor was longer than it should have been. It stretched out like chewing-gum so that by the time I reached the living room again I was tired.

Teta's head was hanging low, covered by her hands. 'Allah have mercy,' came her muffled voice. 'Why doesn't He take me? Who needs an old woman? Why take the boy?'

I stood for minutes or hours stroking my shirt, feeling the softness of my belly beneath Naji's hardening blood. Then I crept over to Teta and touched her cheek.

'It's not your fault,' I said. And I was crying.

Chapter Eighteen

It was dark when I was woken up and led home beneath a sky filled with a million stars. Mami and Papi, limp and tired, had come back without Naji. They'd left him somewhere alone. As Mami led me through the house, the air was heavy with unsaid things, and I climbed into my bed and slept.

Sharp voices woke me in the night, prickly as thorns. Still fuzzy with sleep, I crept down the corridor towards their bedroom. The door was ajar.

'I hardly remember myself,' I could hear Mami saying, 'but I was ordinary, sometimes happy and sometimes sad like any other human being. It's only since you left us that everything's changed. I don't know what we've become, or what I've become. I don't know myself any longer.'

Sleep had gone from my head now. The bed-warmth was leaving me, and beneath my bare feet the floor was cold. Except for the glow that came from their room, the house was still and dark.

I saw Papi reach up and touch Mami's cheek. '*I* know you.' But she turned away sharply.

'And now you hate me too,' said Papi softly. 'Naji was right when he said that.'

Quick as a snake, Mami snatched his hair with both hands, grasping it in clenched fists. She shook him by the head. 'Stop feeling sorry for yourself! Every morning you wake up and find it out afresh. You walk the same circle again and again, when my boy, my son . . .' There was a choking sound and she unhooked her hands from Papi's hair. 'If it weren't for you he wouldn't be lying there with a face like a corpse.'

I saw Naji's face again, not as I'd known it for eight years, but as it had been that last moment, all floppy and hanging, a loose eyelash on one cheek.

'He's my son too, Aida. Don't forget that.'

Mami collapsed into his chest, sobbing.

'We'll go and see him tomorrow,' said Papi.

'But what if he . . . ?'

Papi stroked her hair. 'He won't.'

Mami's eyes were red and puffy. 'Who trusts what any doctor says? What do words mean?' She started to cry again. 'Didn't you see him? The blood, his leg, his face?' She sat down heavily on the bed.

'Mami?'

She didn't hear me, so pushing open the door, I went and buried my head in the soft place between her shoulder and breast. 'Where is he? Where's Naji?'

She blinked to clear her eyes. 'In hospital, my love.'

I pulled away to look at her. 'Isn't he dead?'

She hugged me to her. 'No, my love, he isn't dead.'

Her arms tightened round me till my bones hurt. It was a beautiful, wonderful pain.

* * *

172

Early the following day, with slamming doors, a hurry of footsteps and the soft chatter of voices, Uncle Wadih arrived. But there was no jumping or running this time, no helping with bags from the boot of the cream Mercedes. Teta cried, Papi hugged him tight, and Mami put her hand to her chest. He squatted to kiss me and pinch my cheek, then went inside to talk to Papi. The smell of wood and spice followed him as he floated away like a man walking through water.

I caught words through the door: 'A piece of metal lodged in his leg . . . he lost a lot of blood . . . unconscious . . . Idiots, all of them, burn their religion!'

When the door opened again Uncle was sitting on the sofa smoking, his legs crossed. He held out his hands for me to go to him, and I went.

'What, as slowly as an ant? Don't you want to welcome your uncle?' He sat me beside him. 'You're worried about your brother, *ha*?' And when I nodded, 'Don't you worry, he'll get better.'

'Where's Papi gone?'

'To the bank. He has to get money to pay the hospital.'

'Will there be enough? Will they leave the metal in Naji's leg because we're poor?'

Uncle put his arm round my shoulders and pulled me close. 'Didn't I tell you not to worry?'

Mami and Papi went to the hospital, and me and Uncle and Teta stayed behind. Teta fed us sweet melon and dark plums as flies whirred round the table.

'Have you been eating well down there, my son?' she asked, spooning more melon onto Uncle's plate.

'How do you find me?' He leant back for her to see. 'Not a kilo more or less than before.'

'But how are you managing to get food? Where from, when people are starving?'

'One manages.' He took a big bite and wiped a drip from his chin with his finger-like thumb.

I spat out a plum stone. 'Uncle, did you see a building collapse in Beirut?'

'Yes, more than one.'

'Were there any children in it?'

He exchanged a look with Teta before shaking his head. 'No.'

'We saw planes fighting in the sky over there.' I pointed through the wall.

'Mm.' He nodded. Then to Teta: 'The Israeli Air Force brought down about ninety Syrian planes in the last week or two, and *they* didn't lose a single one. Their army's driven the Syrians from Jezzine.'

'And the Palestinians?' asked Teta.

'They're leaving from Beirut and Trablos by sea, thousands of them. Arafat will soon follow.'

'Good. God speed.' Teta snatched at a fly. 'But son, what were you still doing down there in all this mess?'

Uncle carried on chewing.

'Wadih?'

He swallowed. 'I'm here now, aren't I?'

Teta sighed. 'And now Naji.' She looked up at the ceiling and thumped her chest. 'Naji, my soul. God keep him.'

Three hours later it seemed that God had heard and decided to keep him, because when Mami walked in her mouth was soft. Then she smiled, which meant that Naji was going to be all right.

* * *

174

Although they never let me go with them, Mami and Papi went to the hospital every day; and when the day came two weeks later for Naji to come home, Papi said he would go alone to fetch him.

Money passed between Uncle and Papi that morning, a big wad of it that made Papi object and try to give some back, but Uncle refused. 'There's more, plenty more. I know you don't have any left, and this is nothing to me. Take it.'

'But where did you get it from? So much of it.'

'*Yalla*,' replied Uncle, patting Papi's arm. 'Go and bring your son home.'

After Papi had left, Mami went to prepare Naji's room, while Uncle went straight to the phone to make a call. 'It's business,' he said, and shut the door behind him.

Teta paced about the house. Then she tried to start lunch, but soon gave up. 'I can't think,' she said, putting her hand to her head, 'not even to cook. I don't know what I'm doing.'

Her restlessness made me jittery too, and I wished Uncle would get off the phone. I wanted to talk to him. I wanted to ask him how Naji would be when he came back. Would he look the same? First he'd been dead and then he wasn't. Would it be like having a ghost for a brother? Uncle would explain.

I opened the dining-room door and put my head round to see if he was off the phone yet, but he wasn't.

'The Ottoman citadel at Sayda,' he was saying, 'or in Soor, or Burj el Shmali, wherever you like. Stick your shovel in any hillside in the country and something will fall out. Don't you know that already?' The sharpness of his voice surprised me. 'Exactly. Just get there before the militia do or we'll have to pay them.'

175

Then Teta was behind me. 'Leave your uncle to his business,' she said, pulling the door softly shut again.

'But what am I supposed to do?' I asked.

'We'll just sit down and wait.' Teta turned round one way, then the other. 'No – no, I can't sit here for the next two hours waiting.' She thought a moment. 'It's quiet out now. We'll go somewhere.'

'But I'm not allowed to.'

'You'll be with me. I'll tell your mother, don't worry. We'll go and visit my friend, make sure she's all right. The bombs have been falling her side of the valley all week.'

'Is it more dangerous there?'

Teta nodded. 'Her house faces the shelling.'

My heart beat less fast this time as Teta and I walked up the hill and along the high road. The shelling was further away today, a dull rumble like the quarrying in the forest.

Teta squinted in the strong sun, her cheeks bunched high, a loose strand of hair waggling near her ear as she walked. 'It makes you think,' she puffed, 'what happened to your brother – it makes you think about those who lose their children, what they must feel.'

At first I thought she was talking about the dust girl, who must have had parents, and perhaps brothers and sisters too.

But Teta was thinking of someone else. 'My friend lost her daughter,' she said.

'Amal's mother? But she must have been grown-up.'

Teta tipped back her head. 'No. They're always children, never mind how big they get.'

Teta's friend was kneeling near the flowerbed when we arrived, her broad white back to us. I couldn't see her face, but her hands were working, thick hands that pressed down on the earth round some marigolds to make them stand up straighter. When she heard us, it took her a minute to get up, but there was no smile. She only nodded and waved us closer with a trembling hand. 'Welcome, welcome. *Ahlan.*' And I didn't feel afraid.

She eased herself straight, the creases in her shirt smoothing out as her flesh settled. There was a solidness about her that seemed rooted to the earth, a heaviness as if she carried an invisible load. Those feet in their open-toed slippers couldn't possibly ever have jumped or hopped or skipped.

We walked towards the house, and this time the old woman didn't make any attempt to touch me. I glanced up into the mulberry tree as we passed, but there was no fruit on it now.

'So you come again, and bring your little girl, God keep her. What was her name now?'

Teta reminded her.

She nodded. 'I'm going to make coffee. You'll drink with me.'

Mami wouldn't like this kitchen, I thought. It wasn't too clean. With a bucket full of soapy water, she would inch her way round it with her cloths, leaving streaks of sparkling water behind her. Yet Teta sat at the table and said nothing about it.

As her friend balanced the *rakweh* on the stove, she said, 'Go and find Amal, my girl. Run and find her. She's on the veranda at the back,' and waved towards the back of the house.

I stood a moment, uncertain. Part of me wanted to stay and hear what they would say to each other, but I obeyed her shaking arm and went.

The room I stepped into was large and empty. Two windows looked onto the yard, and sunlight flooded in round a vine to lie in mottled strips across the stone floor, showing up small balls of dust. Mami wouldn't like that either. This should have been the dining room, but there was no table and only one chair with an *argeel* standing on the floor next to it.

It wasn't until I reached the doorway at the far end of the room that a bubble burst in my head the way it does when you understand something suddenly, and I laughed out loud, wishing that Karim were here. He would know that it hadn't been a ghost he'd seen in the window surrounded by mist, but the old woman sitting on the only chair in the room smoking her hubble-bubble.

The corridor led to a veranda that ran the whole length of the house, with doors opening onto it, and outside, Amal was standing against the railings fingering a hole in the metal made by shrapnel. For a moment I thought I heard the softest humming, but when she turned round I wasn't so sure. Running over, she grabbed my hands, held them upright and started clapping against them.

I joined in but couldn't go as fast as her and said so.

A huge smile appeared on her face but she didn't stop. Then the happiness moved down her arms, making the clapping faster, and my hands lost the rhythm.

For the next half-hour, we ran races from one end of the veranda to the other, coloured in a big book she had and played more clapping games. I noticed that shrapnel had studded the walls, and an outer corner of the veranda had been blasted away. Below us too, there were gaps in the trees where bombs had landed.

Finally we stood looking out over the valley that fell below us and rose again on the far side into tall mountains. Houses dotted the dark green slopes, and the cicadas hissed and throbbed from their hiding-places. A dog ran across a yard far below, someone shouted, and a baby cried. A truck swerved round a sharp corner, throwing up clouds of dust behind it. Piled on its open back were potatoes or apples, and a man beside them who hung on, shouting through a loudspeaker. But the name of the fruit or vegetable thinned like mist across the valley until it was too fine to make out.

I turned to Amal. 'What's your favourite fruit? Mine's apricots. Naji's too. He's my brother, you know.' Naji and I had agreed that apricots were the best fruit: the smell and colour and squash of them, then smashing the stone open to eat the nut. 'What's your favourite? Cherries?'

She shook her head, fetched the book we'd coloured in and drew the fruit.

'A lemon? *Lemons* are your favourite fruit?'

Beaming, she wrote down a word.

'Yes, I like them with sugar too. Mami cuts them in half and we put lots of sugar on top and lick it off. Is that what you do? And when the sugar goes, we put more on – Mami doesn't know it but we do.'

I drew another lemon next to hers.

'Naji ate one once standing on his head. He's in hospital now because he got shot and maybe he died for a while too, but he's coming home today.' My thoughts glistened with happiness. 'I thought he was never coming back, but now he is!'

I looked up at the pale blue sky.

'What colour do you like best?'

The colouring pencil she picked was yellow.

'Like lemons, or . . . like the sun!' I sighed. 'I like mauve best. I used to like orange but now I like mauve. It was that lesson about the sea and the snails that changed my mind – how they got mauve out of the snails, even though the snails live in the sea and the sea's blue.'

I laughed at the silliness of it. The excitement of knowing Naji would be home was making me giddy.

'I like the word too. Mauve.' I let it float away into the sky. 'Mauvy-moovy-marvy-meevy-marvy-moovy-movy-marvy.' I giggled. 'This-colour-that-colour-boo-colour-do-colour-why-colour-which-colour. Can you say that? Can you?'

I stopped laughing. Naji would be able to say it, but he might not want to. He might still not be talking to me. If only two more hours had passed and he was at home, I could see him and know. Would he speak to me, or would he be silent like Amal?

'Can you say it? Say it! Please say it!'

Even if she could, she didn't. She scrambled to her feet and ran into the house.

I sat up. I'd upset her.

Following her inside, I headed down a new passage but didn't get far. One of the rooms off it made me stop. It was different from the others, a bedroom furnished with old wooden furniture that was carved round the edges and legs. There must have been more furniture here than in any other room in the house: a bed and wardrobe and dresser and bedside table. The bed was made with clean sheets and a coverlet, and on the table was a glass of marigolds. I went in and opened the wardrobe door. There were dresses inside it, a young woman's colourful dresses, and below them, lined up at the bottom of the wardrobe, several pairs of heeled shoes.

I carried on down the passage and through the one-chair dining room. In the kitchen, the old woman was handing Amal a speckled yellow pear. 'Eat, my soul, eat your fill and may you never want for anything.'

I received an apple, small and green but sweet, and we stood in the cool kitchen eating. This time I didn't worry about the food.

'This is nothing,' the old woman said to Teta, as if carrying on from a conversation they'd been having. 'I was born into poverty like this, that's no punishment. Not for what I've done.'

'What's this talk?' Teta waved a dismissive hand. 'Forget the past and let it lie where it belongs. We have enough to do surviving the present.'

'And I cut up your heart because . . . because of something I did.' She squinted. 'Was it to do with your son? Yes, it was because of . . . of something.' Her eyes were moist.

'Because of nothing. Wadih's content and that's all.'

'That's right. I remember. My daughter wanted to marry him. I remember it now. She came and told me, and when I said no, she cried.'

'Stop it, *ya* Latifeh.'

The old woman looked questioningly at Teta. 'Is that why she died?'

Teta stood and held out a hand to Amal. 'Come. Yes, you're a young lady now, aren't you?' She gave her a smile. 'You must look after your grandmother, do you hear?'

Amal nodded.

Uncle Wadih had wanted to marry Amal's mother? *My* Uncle Wadih? But that would have made Amal my cousin. Once I'd thought that Amal was strange and that her grandmother was a witch, but now our families were joined somehow.

As the two women said their goodbyes, Amal made me play one last clapping game in the yard. I was winning when something touched the top of my head, something big and with a weight to it. The old woman's hand rested on me a moment, shivering, before it fell back to her hip. I lost the clapping game.

After we'd crossed the yard and were on the road, I could still feel the pressure of her rough hand on my head. 'Teta, doesn't she get tired of shaking her hands so much?'

'No. Well, I don't know, maybe she does, but it's not her doing it, just the way her body is.' She stopped to look back. 'Do you see the care for the dead? Look what she does for her daughter.'

I turned and searched the yard. 'What?'

'The marigolds, child. Nothing but marigolds, because her daughter loved them.'

When we got back, a smell of cooking was coming from the kitchen, and Teta went to help Mami with lunch.

Uncle was in the living room reading the newspaper.

'Uncle?' There was so much to ask him.

'Yes?' he drawled.

'When you were younger, were you really going to marry Amal's mother?'

I might as well have let off a firecracker next to his ear, he looked so startled.

'Amal?'

'They live on the high road. The house with the fountain.'

He closed the paper and adjusted his pale pink shirt sleeves. His face had lost its calmness.

'*Were* you going to marry her?'

He sat back heavily. 'The only woman I was ever going to marry,' he said at last.

But then she'd died, I knew that, and Uncle must have been sad.

'What would have happened if you'd married her?'

He stared at the floor so long I thought he had frozen.

'Uncle?'

His words came slowly, not in the voice he used for children, or the one he used for women, or even for men. It was a voice I'd never heard before, a dead sort of voice.

'If I'd married her everything would have been different,' he told the floor. 'I would have stayed here in Ein Douwra, lived here and looked after the shop instead of your father. And he wouldn't have gone down to Beirut that day.' He took a deep breath. 'Everything would have been different.'

Chapter Nineteen

I went outside to wait for Naji. It was quiet on the veranda, and the Rose Man's roses were lit up in the sun, balancing motionless on long stems. I didn't understand how life could be any different from how it was now. Yet Uncle had seemed so sad and strange, as if he could see exactly how it would have been.

I put my nose into an enormous dark red rose and breathed in. It smelt of candy-floss, or honey dropped in cool water, and had opened so wide that the tiny yellow stalks in the centre showed. Closing my eyes, I was filled slowly with happiness. 'Naji's coming home,' I whispered. The petals tickled my cheek, but when I opened my eyes again, their redness shocked me. They looked like blood-soaked paper, and the sweeter-than-honey scent was sickly.

Just then the clunk of Papi's car told me they'd arrived, and I ran to see.

Naji was asleep in the back. It was Papi who carried him inside, with Uncle behind bringing the crutches. Teta wrung her hands, and after Mami fussed about moving pillows and pulling back sheets, they laid him on his bed.

This Naji was thinner and paler than the one I knew, his hair a little longer. 'He needs to rest, *ya habib albi*,' Teta whispered, her eyes growing shiny at the sight of his right leg, which was a cocoon of bandages. 'Look how they've smashed him up.'

'But your dreams were wrong, Teta. He didn't die.'

'No.' She seemed puzzled. 'No, he didn't die.'

Leaving him to rest, we moved to the living room.

'There was bleeding inside his thigh,' said Papi as he sat down. 'The doctor said that if it had clotted, and if the clots had moved through his body to his lungs . . . He was lucky.'

Uncle stood silently, looking out of the window at the rosebushes. Mami was watching him.

'Did the doctor say anything else?' she asked.

'He gave him some medicine to help him sleep for an hour or so,' replied Papi.

'But about walking, I mean.'

The lines between Papi's eyebrows deepened. 'It'll take six months to heal, maybe longer.'

'But he'll be able to walk again, won't he, son?' said Teta.

'He'll walk, but he may have a limp.' Raising a foot from the floor, Papi dragged it forward with the toes still on the ground. 'Like that.'

Mami spoke from beneath her hand. 'The doctor said that?'

'Yes.'

Uncle turned back from the window. The packet of cigarettes he picked up from the tray wasn't the sort he usually smoked, but he took it anyway and headed out onto the veranda.

I spent the next hour wandering to and from Naji's open door. Then I gathered his favourite possessions into a small pile beside his bed: a bagful of Lego pieces, his painted plastic soldiers, a book about tanks and aeroplanes, a funny-shaped pebble, a silver bicycle bell. I listened to him breathing, and wondered how things would be when he woke up.

I touched his leg gently with one finger. Somewhere underneath, I didn't know where, there was a hole. I touched the arm that lay on top of the sheets. It felt soft but didn't move, just like the last time I'd touched it when he fell. He hadn't moved then either. I was suddenly filled with a fear that he would never wake up, and that the silence between us would continue for ever, whitening down the years.

Hours later, I was still sitting on the floor beside his crutches when he opened his eyes and turned sleepily towards me. He blinked. Then he smiled. 'Did you see me get shot?' His voice sounded rusty, but that didn't matter.

'Yes, I saw.' I could barely speak, I was so happy. 'Look, I put your toys here so you could reach.'

He leant down to feel his bandaged leg.

'Does it hurt a lot?'

'Not as much as in hospital. They did an X-ray there, and I saw a black-and-white picture of my bones.'

'Is the bullet still in there?'

'No, they took it out. But there's a metal stick now to hold my bone together.'

'Can you feel it?'

'No. They said it might never come out, but I'll be able to walk with it in.' He shrugged, then closed his eyes and was asleep again.

It seemed he didn't know about the dragging toes.

For the next two days Naji stayed in bed. He slept and sweated and occasionally moaned. When he woke he complained that he felt sick, and Mami said it must be the medicine. But on the third day he felt better.

'Thank God,' sighed Teta as she watched him sit up in bed. 'Nabeel was going to crack into pieces soon.'

'Yes.' Mami smiled. Since Naji had come home, she'd been acting softer towards Papi. And it wasn't just me Naji had started talking to again but Papi, who seemed more alive because of it.

Teta nodded. 'We've finished with death, so I can go to my grave in peace.'

Mami gave a little smile but said nothing.

'I brought Naji some blessed incense.' Teta showed her a sachet with a piece of cotton wool in it covered with something brown and grainy. It looked as if it had come from inside the priest's ear. She handed it to me. 'Take it to your brother.'

I opened it and sniffed. It smelt churchy.

Naji was reading in bed. He didn't think much of the incensy cotton wool, and when I asked him to tell me about the hospital he didn't want to.

'But what did the doctor say?'

'He said I lost a lot of blood,' he murmured, 'and that the bullet missed a big vein. The doctor said people can die from being shot in the leg, and that I was lucky.'

'Those boys you were playing with,' I began, but he stopped me sharply.

'I don't want to speak about them ever again, understand?'

'But I—'

'Ever!'

There was a knock on the door, and a few minutes later Uncle Wadih brought Ghada and Samira in.

'We've come to see you.' Ghada smiled. 'How are you doing, Naji?'

Samira clasped her cheeks. 'Look what they've done to him, *ya* Ghada, look.'

'Don't worry, he'll be swinging on those crutches like a monkey soon,' laughed Uncle, but for once Naji didn't find him funny.

Ghada's eyes wandered up and down Naji's body, stopping at his white leg. 'How could such a terrible thing happen in our town?'

She settled herself on the bed at his feet, which Naji didn't like, while Samira took a chair.

'You're feeling bad, aren't you?' asked Samira. 'In pain.'

'It's okay,' replied Naji, frowning.

'I understand.' Samira nodded understandingly. 'I get spells like that too. I can barely walk in a straight line at times, I feel so weak. Ghada has the same problem, but with her it's not nerves, it's shoes. If she wasn't so concerned with fashionable shoes that don't fit her, she could walk faster and straighter. But when Ghada wears heels, she walks sideways like a crab.'

I saw Uncle try not to smile.

'Samira!' cried Ghada.

'It's true, sister, you know it is. And then there's our father. Each morning he spends a quarter of an hour plotting and navigating the best way to get out of bed.'

They carried on like that for a while, then turned to Uncle.

'We're glad you've come up again,' said Ghada.

'Yes, it's on the television,' said her sister. 'That's no place to live. Not that we're much better off here. The last few weeks,' she shook her head, 'if only they'd let a body get some sleep.'

'Nowhere's safe,' said Uncle. 'But in Beirut no one takes notice of the guns any more. We go out between rounds of artillery fire. There are gunmen shooting from building to building. From my window I can see the glint of the binoculars on their rifles.'

Ghada looked frightened, and Uncle's tone grew lighter.

'But I have this little plant in the kitchen, and I talk to it. That way they think there's someone else there. Because if they see that you live alone, who knows? So I talk to my plant.'

Which made everyone laugh.

That afternoon Uncle and Papi stood outside the living-room window drinking coffee and talking. Inside, Naji and I were cutting strings of men and women out of newspaper as the smell of Mami boiling white vests drifted in from the kitchen.

'Women don't understand, or shouldn't,' I heard Uncle say. 'Why should they know about the filth that men do? Our country's become a hell on earth: the hooded men at checkpoints, the kidnappings and car bombs. And the lists of the dead grow so long they can't be counted. What are we approaching now? Twenty thousand dead since June it must be, and nearly all civilians. The smell of rotting flesh in Beirut, *ya* Nabeel – they're dumping corpses in the sea because there's nowhere else to put them.'

I held up my string of women, blackened with words. Opposite me, Naji was staring at the scissors.

There was more talking that was too low to hear, then: 'The PLO have left Lebanon,' Papi said. 'It's what we've been waiting and hoping for.'

'Yes,' replied Uncle, 'after eleven hours of bombing in one day.'

'But the killing of children – the schools and orphanages and hospitals – how could Israel have hit so many? How?'

The scent of bleach from the kitchen was thin and silver, almost painful.

'My brother, the Israelis have equipment that can target whatever they choose. They have some of the best pilots in the world and they've bombed the whole of West Beirut into a garbage dump. People are living among rubbish and death.' A coffee-cup clinked against its saucer. 'And from the very first children's hospitals were hit, children's mental asylums too. God can only imagine . . .'

I didn't want Naji to hear this. I hadn't told him about his dragging leg, or about what had happened to Papi in Beirut. Since he'd been shot, something had changed. I wanted to keep him safe.

A short while later more conversation drifted in.

'But dropping cluster bombs and phosphorus grenades that burn the flesh off a living person,' said Papi. 'What sort of a death is that for a child?'

'What sort of death is it for anyone? They've cut our supplies too. There's no electricity, no anaesthetic, no food or water. And it's hot as hell itself in Beirut.'

Papi didn't seem to hear him. 'Who will judge those who kill children?'

The stove in the kitchen hissed as water spattered onto it.

Pushing back his chair and grabbing the crutches, Naji hobbled off into his bedroom. I found him beside his artillery canister. Leaning forward to scoop out a handful, he fingered a jagged piece of shrapnel, a long silver bullet, a red cartridge.

'What's the matter? Is something missing?' I asked.

He dropped the pieces, clinking, back into the canister. 'No. Only I don't want them any more.'

'What? But you spent ages collecting them!'

'Well now I don't want them. They can be thrown away.'

'Are you joking, Naji?'

He shook his head. 'I'm going to take the canister across the road and leave it by the rubbish drums.'

'You can't. I mean, with your leg. I'll take it.'

'Papi can do it.'

'I don't mind. I can roll it.'

I took a step forward, but Naji put out an arm to stop me. 'No, Papi'll do it.'

I was sent to fetch Papi. When he came in, he didn't say a word, just looked at Naji. Then he replaced the canister lid and lifted it up. Metal clanked as the pieces rolled and settled. The weight showed in Papi's stiff legs as he walked down the corridor.

Naji hobbled to the window to watch.

Nothing more was said about it, only when Papi came back, he had a little smile on his face.

Shelling woke me in the night. When I got up to go to the bathroom, a light was on in Naji's room.

I padded over.

A candle stood on the bedside table, and Papi, still as a tree, was looking down at Naji. The wobbling circle of light

191

showed Naji's face gleaming with sweat. He groaned softly in his sleep as if something hurt.

Papi reached down. For a moment his hand hovered over Naji's head. Then, as softly as one would touch a soap bubble, he stroked the damp hair, the forehead, Naji's cheek. Then he drew back his hand and his body began to shudder. I had never seen him cry before.

Standing there, I wished that the witch really was a witch and that Papi had been cursed. A spell could be broken to make him well. Now, though, there was no way to save him.

Chapter Twenty

One morning in mid-September, the world stopped moving. No trucks or cars drove up the hill, no cockerels crowed, no birds chirped. Not a cat, dog or insect moved.

Mami and Papi stood facing the radio as if it were a television. Uncle stood on the veranda leaning against the railings with his head bent low, and Naji was sitting in front of an untouched breakfast, his hands flat on either side of the plate.

'What is it?' I whispered. 'What happened?'

He frowned and strained to hear the radio better. 'They killed him – Jumayyil – the one who was going to be president.'

'They killed the president?'

'He wasn't president yet, but they killed him anyway.'

For the rest of the morning, Mami ironed in silence. Uncle, who hadn't shaved, sat talking to Papi, and Papi slumped lower than ever in his chair.

It wasn't until the afternoon when the bombs started falling as usual that Uncle had the heart to watch me do forward rolls, backward rolls and bad cartwheels. But when the phone rang, he closed the dining-room door so he could speak in private. A few minutes later he was back and gave Naji a wink. 'How about some ice-cream? I'll go and buy a big tub. What flavours do you like?'

'Pistachio.'

'Yes,' I agreed, even though I preferred chocolate.

'You're going to go out under the shells and bullets for ice-cream?' asked Papi. The air was cracking and shaking now.

'The children want ice-cream. Naji's been sitting here bored and sick for a week.'

'You're feeling better, aren't you, Naji?' Papi asked with a smile.

Smiling back, Naji nodded.

'Still, let me get them something to sweeten their teeth. Anyway, I have to pass by the post office.'

'Today?' asked Mami. 'Now?'

'They'll be open. I have to make a phone call abroad.'

'Be careful,' Mami said. 'Be careful.'

As he was about to leave, there was a knock at the door.

Juhaina and Mami kissed each other on the cheeks three times – *mwah*, *mwah*, *mwah* – although Juhaina only kissed air. Then Mami introduced her to Uncle in the kitchen.

'You never told me what glamorous friends you have, Aida,' Uncle said, holding Juhaina's hand and examining her calmly. 'Now I feel sorry that I'm on my way out.'

Juhaina laughed, pleased. 'You're Aida's brother-in-law? But . . . so different from your brother.'

Uncle gave a little bow. 'Perhaps next time we'll meet for longer.'

'Ah, no, unfortunately.' Juhaina explained that she was leaving Lebanon.

'Then you've come to say your goodbyes.' He tutted regretfully. 'Whichever way you turn in life, you come across lost possibilities.'

When Uncle had left, Juhaina was led into the living room. After flashing her teeth at me and Naji, she looked about her in a way that made me embarrassed about the house and the things in it. She looked at Papi in exactly the same way.

'No, please, don't get up,' she said, 'I'm not going to stay long.' With an uneasy glance at the stain on his forehead, the jewelly hand touched his quickly and was drawn back.

She looked funny here. Either she had grown larger or she'd made the house shrink round her. As she sat, rearranging her skirt over her crossed legs, and the gold bangles on her wrists, Papi took her in from top to toe with one look.

Mami talked with her for a while about what had happened that morning.

'It was the last straw,' said Juhaina. 'Of course, we'd already decided to leave, but today confirmed it.'

'Yes,' said Mami. 'It's so terrible I can't believe it yet.'

After a little more talk, Juhaina said, 'I heard what happened to your son' – she swept an arm to where Naji was sitting – 'and I thanked God it wasn't mine.'

Mami told me to go and put some water on to heat.

'Don't let the child make Arabic coffee, Aida,' Juhaina said as I passed. 'I don't drink it unless I'm forced to. I only drink Nescafé.'

When I came back Juhaina was still talking. 'At first I told Fareed I didn't want to leave. "You don't want to leave?" he said to me. "With your nerves? You can barely stand up any longer." But you know how it is: we've lived here all our lives.'

'Everyone wants to leave,' said Mami. 'You're lucky that you're able to.'

'Well, what to do?' Juhaina smoothed an eyebrow. 'They've driven us out of our own houses and our own country, and ruined my nervous system into the bargain.'

Mami got up to make the coffee. 'Sugar?' she asked.

'No, *chérie*, I'm always watching my figure. Fareed brings home sweets and I send them back out again.'

For a long time there was no sound except the ripping of threads as Naji picked the frayed ends of his bandages, and the occasional *tink* of gold bangles.

'I've passed by your shop once or twice,' said Juhaina finally, not looking at Papi.

'Yes, Aida told me.'

Juhaina wet her lips. 'She's a good woman to be working up there all summer in the heat.'

He nodded, and I watched Juhaina's wary sideways glances at him, as if he might jump on her at any moment. They both seemed relieved when Mami came back in. She asked where Juhaina was travelling to.

'Canada. Fareed's managed to sort things out. As I say, I wasn't keen to go but . . . look at the situation you're in, for example. What would I do if something like that happened to my child? I don't know how I could live with myself.' She smoothed a crease in her skirt.

'No,' said Papi suddenly. 'I don't know how you could live with yourself either.'

Juhaina started in surprise, but a moment later the conversation continued. 'As I was saying, I don't ask how Fareed managed it, I just thank God he did. He knows all sorts of high-up people. And he's got a sister out there in

Canada, so at least I'll have someone.' She sighed and looked sorry for her Canada self.

I picked up a long rubber band and started flicking the table.

'"I don't like the cold," I told Fareed, "you know I don't."
But one has to make sacrifices, *n'est-ce pas*?' She glanced at Naji, her eyes resting on his leg. 'I have to think of my son. I can't let him grow up like that, can I?'

Naji stopped picking at his bandages.

'There are worse ways of growing up,' said Papi quietly. 'If your parents are imbeciles, for example.'

There was a long silence.

'Um, that's true, yes,' said Juhaina at last. 'Still, I – I don't know how we shall cope.'

'Aren't you glad to be going?' I asked.

'What's that, my love?' Juhaina's teeth flashed again as she turned towards me. 'Yes, of course I'm glad. *Je suis aux anges.* But you know, Aida, I can't even take all my things with me. My furniture, my carpets, the bits and pieces round the house. And I'll have to send the maid back.' She shook her head till her earrings tinkled. 'I don't know, *chérie*, I don't know how I shall manage.'

Mami forced a smile. 'You'll be happy there, you'll see.'

'I'll send for them later maybe. That's what I'll do.'

'For the maid?' asked Papi.

Juhaina showed us her teeth again. 'No, of course not. There are enough of those in Canada, I bet.' The toes of her crossed leg moved in a circle. 'But perhaps the war won't last and I'll be able to come back and fetch them myself. It can't last much longer. I mean, how many more months can they keep going on this way?'

'Months?' Papi leant forward. 'You think it'll be over in months?'

I stopped flicking the rubber band.

'It's going to take more than months, isn't it, Papi?' said Naji.

Papi's face eased as he nodded.

'Can I get you something else, Juhaina?' Mami asked, but her friend raised a hand.

'I know as well as anyone what's happening, both in Beirut and here,' she announced. 'The country's become a slaughterhouse – like they slaughter pigs and cows, that's what they're doing to people now.' She waved towards the window. 'Can't you hear? No, Aida, *c'est trop*, even for me. Without a brave heart in my chest, I wouldn't be stepping out of my door at all.'

'Yes, I know, you have to be strong. Everyone does. Can I get you another coffee?'

Juhaina shook her head. 'But don't be offended, it's not your coffee. It's powdered milk I can't stand. It makes my stomach turn. At least we'll have fresh milk in Canada. One has to count the good things.'

'Yes, you'll have fresh milk *and* your family won't be slaughtered,' muttered Papi.

For the first time, Juhaina looked directly at him, her mouth opening and shutting.

Mami got to her feet. 'There's cordial. Or something to eat, maybe.'

But Juhaina tucked her handbag under her arm. 'No, I've got to be going.' She ran light fingers over her stiff hair. 'I have so much to do it makes me dizzy.'

'Goodbye,' I said as she got up. I was glad that the woman who knew when a bird farted was leaving for good.

Her heels clicked across the kitchen floor then stopped. 'Will your son walk again?' came her voice in a loud whisper. 'Take him abroad, Aida, that's what I would do. Cripples are treated better abroad.'

There were three kisses again, the jangle of car keys, some more goodbyes, then silence.

Naji was staring at Papi. 'Am I going to be a cripple?'

Although the creases lining Papi's forehead grew deeper, he didn't answer.

'Am I, Papi? Am I going to be like the man with no legs who sits outside the church? The one in the wheelchair?'

'No.' Papi sounded sure. 'You're not going to be a cripple. You won't ever be like that man.'

Mami came back in. She went up to Papi and they stood facing each other. There was going to be shouting and arguing.

I didn't know what it was at first. It sounded like someone spraying out a mouthful of water. Then I saw. It was Mami. With one hand held flat against her stomach, she bent backwards and allowed her laughter to float up to the ceiling.

Papi looked frightened. Naji's mouth hung open. The sound of such laughter in the house was a strange thing. The way it bubbled up like water, like silver, low at first, then louder and faster. It carried on until Mami was red-faced and gasping for air. She wiped her eyes. 'What a friend!'

Papi's face lifted and suddenly he looked young. He didn't take his eyes from Mami as she laughed again, lightly this time.

'You remember her party?' said Mami. 'It was terrible. The people there were more interested in the clothes on their bodies than the words in their mouths. And then she comes here. Those things she said! She should never have said such things. Talking like that about leaving, about Canada and . . . and—'

'It's my fault,' said Papi.

I thought I'd misheard, but then Mami started to shake with laughter again. The bright sun rippled over her shiny black hair. Her laughter swirled round, bouncing off the walls and ceiling. And in the centre of it she stood quivering and shuddering, her mouth open to let it all out, eyes squeezed shut.

Now Papi took hold of her arms to stop her fluttering away. Because the shaking was growing stronger, the laughter turning heavier, until gradually her head sank forwards and her face was lost in Papi's chest.

Naji struggled to his feet, and I stopped to watch. Outside, the mortar shells screamed and rumbled, and inside Mami cried and cried into Papi's heart.

'She comes and talks about bread in the starving man's house,' came her muffled voice.

Papi hugged her close, covered her so tight I was scared he would hurt her.

'They're leaving us,' sobbed Mami. 'Everyone's leaving . . . going away to live new lives far away from any of this. There's nothing left here, nothing but death . . . It's as if they're leaving us in a grave.'

Chapter Twenty-one

The following morning I rushed in. 'Mami, can we go and watch?'

She was standing on a step-ladder washing my bedroom window. 'Watch what?'

When I told her, she stopped scrubbing and the sponge in her hand dribbled soapy water onto the carpet. She held her stomach then, without a word, stepped down and walked out of the room. I followed. Papi was just coming into the house.

'Is it true, Nabeel?'

He nodded. 'Yes. They're telling everyone.'

'They're going to drag a man behind a car!' I said. 'Papi, can we go up to the main road later and watch?'

He stared as though a scorpion had come out of my mouth.

Naji was standing behind me. 'Uncle Wadih can take us.'

Mami turned away. 'The child doesn't know what he's saying. Neither of them does.'

'But Papi said they're telling everyone – that's so they can go and watch,' insisted Naji. 'Everyone's going to be there.'

'They're telling people so they can stay in their houses and pray! Only the dogs and cowards will be there, hooting and gibing.' He sank down, tired, into his chair.

'But Papi, it's only a game,' I told him.

Papi breathed heavily. 'A game.' He looked sick. 'They want revenge for yesterday. Nobody's to step out of the house.'

After that Papi couldn't keep still. All morning and into the afternoon he walked, first round the room and then round the veranda.

'But he's a bad man!' said Naji finally, tottering up to Papi on his crutches.

Papi stopped pacing. His voice was tight. 'Do you want to watch a man being murdered?'

I didn't understand. 'Murdered?'

'But he's a bad man,' repeated Naji. 'He's not like us.'

Papi laughed sourly. 'Not like us? *Ach, ya* Naji, what have I taught you?' He thought for a while. 'Maybe this man's like us and maybe he isn't. He's probably a prisoner and for sure not a Christian, but he's a man. And they're going to tie him to the back of a car in the next town and drag him all the way to Beirut. By the time they get here, if God is kind, the man'll be dead.'

When Mami handed Papi a list of food to buy the next morning, she held onto his hand. 'Don't buy any meat, even if you can find it. I haven't the stomach to see or touch it today.'

Papi was still out and Naji asleep in his room when Uncle came over to use the telephone. Through the closed dining-room door his voice rose and fell as Mami and I carried in some washing. Then he began to shout.

'What kind of a delay is this?' came Uncle's angry voice. 'By the time you bring them, the war will be over and I'll be in an old people's home! There are others who'll do this work, don't forget that, and probably do it better and quicker. I don't have to depend on you. There are a thousand others like you, so don't think you can keep me sweet with your excuses because I won't wait.'

Mami, who was walking down the corridor ahead of me with a basket of clothes, stopped to listen, so I stopped too.

'How? *You*'re asking *me* how? My brother, listen. Just take an iron rod, dig about a bit in the earth near the tombs and when you find the edge of a slab, work your way round it. Yes – yes, there'll be a cut in the stone somewhere.' He paused. 'How should I know? That's how the Romans made their graves . . . Why? They didn't want you to find them, that's why.'

The mention of graves reminded me of the ones near the castle in Jbeil, and of how I thought I'd seen Uncle drinking coffee with a strange man at a pavement table. I would ask him when he got off the phone. I'd ask him if he'd really been there.

There was more low talking. Then Uncle's voice rose again. 'On your mother's life, don't let them use dynamite again, do you hear?'

Mami gasped and, with a sudden movement, threw open the door. She stood there shaking, the plastic basket held against her hip, as Uncle replaced the receiver. 'What were you talking about, Wadih? What business are you doing to shame us all?'

'Uncle?'

He turned to me. 'Yes?'

'You were in Jbeil, weren't you? I *did* see you there.'

He smiled. 'What's that, my love?'

203

'When we went to Jbeil with school. Naji went into a shop to buy a dead fish but I was in the street and I saw you.'

He laughed his drumbeat laugh, except now it sounded hollow.

'Wadih?' Mami was still standing there.

Uncle took the basket from her and put it on the floor, then led her gently to a chair. 'You're not going to be angry with me, are you? Not you, Aida, I don't want your anger. It's only work. A man has to work.'

Still clutching my armful of clothes, I watched from the doorway as they sat down close beside each other, their hands almost touching on the table.

'I don't understand.' Mami stared at Uncle's neck. 'What about your proper job?'

He swatted the idea away. 'The company hasn't been working for months. They've already laid off most of their employees. There's no money to pay them.'

'Ruba,' said Mami, 'go and play in your room.'

'Why?'

Uncle shrugged with his mouth. 'Let her stay. Children can judge. Sometimes they make the best judges. Let her decide if what I'm doing is so wrong.'

'But Wadih, what I heard you say on the phone, what you're doing, it's not right.'

'Not right?' Uncle grunted. 'The Europeans came and plundered this land a hundred years ago and now you're telling me we can't do the same? It used to be farmers who found these artefacts as well as archaeologists: they put a spade into the earth and it knocked against some priceless piece of history. And it's still the same. Just think: these people are poor and hungry, and we pay them. Men and boys alike will break into ancient graves for a few lira. All I do is send what they find to places where people at least know its value. Those I deal with in Europe and America aren't poor or stupid: they know and appreciate.'

'You're digging up our history, our wealth, and sending it out of the country?' Mami's hand lay lifeless on the table.

'What would you have me do? Our people need to put bread in their mouths, not gold!'

'But the museums, the government—'

'The museums in Beirut, in Jbeil, everywhere, are being cracked open like nuts and scooped clean.'

He *had* been in Jbeil, then.

'And,' Uncle continued, 'the Lebanese are using bulldozers and cranes to dig up Bronze Age sites. They throw the broken pieces of pottery and stone on rubbish heaps. They destroy the ancient roads and cities beneath their feet. Yes, the government should do something, but it has enough to do. By law these things shouldn't happen. By law anything that's found should be examined by the Department of Antiquities and preserved. But there is no law.' He sat back, rubbing his mouth. 'And the dynamite, you want to know what that's for? They use it to blow open Phoenician sarcophagi! And electric drills, when there's any electricity.' He laughed. 'The fools think there'll be gold and diamonds inside, like in films.'

'I can't believe any of it!' Mami seemed to grow angry. 'I don't understand. Don't you see what you're doing?'

'I know what I see. I see beautiful things, Aida, beautiful things.' He got to his feet. 'Phoenician gold and statues, Byzantine mosaics, daggers and glass bottles the Romans left behind. Everyone who's ever landed here has left something. Little gold pendants with tiny animals inlaid in ivory, rings showing the heads of who knows which emperor. You know how I love beautiful things. So do you. Why should I watch them be destroyed?'

I put down my load of washing on top of Mami's basket. When I looked at her again, she'd taken hold of Uncle's hands and was gazing up at him. 'But it's you who are destroying them,' she said in a low voice.

'No, I'm saving them. Don't beautiful things deserve to be saved? Here, ask your daughter. Ruba, don't beautiful things deserve to be saved?'

'Which beautiful things? The Rose Man thinks his roses are beautiful. Ghada thinks nail polish is beautiful. Naji thinks sports cars are beautiful.'

Uncle burst out laughing. 'See? Wasn't I right? There's a philosopher in every child.'

'Listen to me, Wadih. You can't carry on doing this. It's a crime. Even if no one ever finds out, it's still a crime. And our history—'

'I have as much respect for history as you,' he broke in angrily, 'maybe more, but why shouldn't I make a living out of it? The war's destroyed it anyway. Roman pillars are lying covered with bullet holes, statues broken and scattered in the dirt like garbage. Who's going to save them? And what would the government do with so much history anyway?'

Mami let go of his hands. 'Then you're not the man I thought you were. Not the man I admired or . . .' She flushed. 'Don't you care anything about the past?'

'The past?' I jumped as Uncle pushed his chair to the floor. 'The past has ruined my life, and so has lack of money. It was only money that stopped me marrying her, Aida, only money that kept her from me.'

But his anger passed, and he picked up the chair and sat down again. 'Aida, *ya* Aida,' he said softly, 'there were people in Lebanon once who were gentler than us and more worthy, who had regard for a human being. They buried their children beneath their houses so that they could stay close to them. But life is cheap now, cheaper than a loaf of bread. Why should anyone care about the past? It can't help them.' He was silent for a while. 'Look at my brother. What good has it done him to care about the past?'

Mami hung her head.

'We can't all care as much as he does. We can't all have such a clean heart.'

'No,' replied Mami gently. 'No.'

I didn't want to be in the room any more, with Mami who was unhappy and with Uncle who'd lied about his work; and for once when I asked Mami if I could go out, without even thinking, she said yes.

Grey clouds covered the world, making it airless and damp. As I headed to the main road, a couple of cars passed slowly up the hill, then even more slowly, a truck full of chunks of mountain that left a cloud of dust behind it. But just before I reached the main road, something else caught my attention.

'Look how it's going!'

The rumble of the truck died away, and down a side path, I saw a group of five boys and two girls beside a wall marked with bullet holes. The green-eyed boy and the spotty one were there, but I didn't recognize the others. They were huddled in a circle, shuffling and laughing with excitement. The spotty boy bent down and struggled with something, but he had trouble holding it, and as it kicked I saw it was a cat, a thin black one that didn't like being held.

'Hurry, it's going to shred me!'

One of the girls was untangling a length of string attached to the top of a metal pole sticking up from the ground. 'Okay, okay,' she said, 'I've done it.' And a small brown bird rose up tied to the end of the string.

The grey sky sank lower as the bird bobbed up, pulling first one way then the other, rising and falling in wobbling waves. Then the spotty boy let the cat go. With a yowl, it sprang towards the pole and, standing on its hind legs, waved its paws at the bird.

The flapping grew faster, the string went up, grew tight, and jerked the bird back again. Round and round it flew, its twittering faint among the laughter.

Minutes passed and still I couldn't move.

'Look, it's getting tired.' The boy who spoke was right. The string was growing slack, the fluttering weaker.

A black paw swiped through the air. The cat's tail swung from side to side. A second swipe and the bird was nearly snagged on those claws.

'It's so tired now,' said one of the girls. 'It's not going to last much longer.'

They gathered closer, blocking my view, and suddenly I could move again.

I wanted to scream, to knock them all down and stamp on them. I ran a few steps up the hill for a stone to throw at them, then stopped dead.

I'd never seen the main road so empty before. The nut shop had its shutters pulled down. There were no cars, and only a couple of people in the street. Two men walked towards me talking in low voices but fell silent as they passed. A little way down the road, a young woman with a cloth wrapped round her long hair threw a bucket of water onto the road. Behind her, an older woman came out. The handle of the metal pail she was carrying creaked, and her shoulder was bowed down by its weight. When she reached the roadside, she also tipped out the water, which sloshed and pooled across the tarmac. Then, facing the church, she crossed herself, her lips moving in a prayer before she turned away.

Crying was coming from somewhere. The old man who owned the vegetable shop was standing on the pavement with a bucket on the ground beside him. The crying sound was coming from him. Tugging off his woollen hat, he emptied out his water.

I followed its path. Just there where it spread out, the road was streaked with brown and red. As the water moved, it lifted the colour a little before flowing away into the gutter. A few bubbles swelled and popped in the grate.

The old man's face was squashed into a hundred lines, his eyes hidden deep in two nests of wrinkles. 'They've killed innocence,' he wailed.

I watched a tear ooze from his eye.

'Why?' I asked.

He wiped an arm across his creased face. 'Because he was a Muslim and we're murderers. Because God is asleep and having nightmares.'

As he wept, the air was suddenly pinched and black.

Gesturing to the sky, he called, 'What did that man ever do to anyone?' A trickle of water followed the track of a deep wrinkle. 'He roasted nuts, that's all he did.' The tear reached his white stubble and spread out, zigzagging, between the hairs. 'He roasted nuts.'

'Ruba! Ruba, where are you?'

Mami had seen me run in, and a minute later, the darkness inside the wardrobe leaked out as she opened the door.

'What are you doing in here?' She squatted on her heels, and my tears started again.

'It – it's Ali.'

Sweeping my shoes out onto the floor, she stepped in and sat down beside me. The darkness swelled up round us as she pulled the door shut.

'Ali?' Her breath was soft on my cheek.

'Y-yes. And the bird. He's . . . they've . . .'

She drew my head to her breast and began to stroke it. The smell of her closed round me, a feathery scent of new flowers. When I told her what they'd done, the children and the grown-ups, the stroking stopped. Somewhere under my ear, her heart beat a steady *thud-um, thud-um, thud-um*.

I counted nineteen beats before she spoke. 'Are you sure it was him?'

The tears burnt in my eyes. 'The o-old man told me. He said it was because Ali w-was a Muslim. Is that really why?'

I waited in the darkness. Mami's heart was beating faster now.

'No. They did it because their hearts are black.'

'But he wasn't a bad man. He wasn't any different from us.' A tear washed hot down my cheek. I didn't understand. 'Karim was a Muslim too. I'm glad he's gone.'

Mami was stroking my hair again, firm and hard now. Even now in early autumn, the flowers in her perfume smelt of spring. They would still smell of spring when winter came.

'Mami, people said Ali was a cripple. Will they do the same thing to Naji?'

I heard Mami catch her breath. 'No, my love.' As we sat rocking gently in the dark stillness, she kissed my face.

'Are you going to run away and leave us because you want to be rich and have pretty things?'

Everything but her heart stopped moving. 'Run away?' Now she kissed the top of my head hard. 'No.'

'Mami, will everything be all right again?' It was difficult to swallow. 'Will it?'

'I don't know, my love. When something's broken . . .'

'You mean like the things Uncle was talking about? The treasures?'

She nodded. 'Yes, just like them. Beautiful things get broken too.'

Then she began to sob, and as her tears came, I imagined them flowing down her cheeks, black with kohl.

Papi turned away his face when he heard. Only Naji didn't wince or cry.

'Didn't you hear?' I cried. 'He's dead!'

He swung round. 'So what? He was just . . . just . . . you know.' He stared down at his white leg a moment, then hobbled to his room and closed the door.

The earth had started to shake again when Papi and Mami went into their bedroom. The sound of her crying and his soft voice came from inside.

In my own room, I found the glass eye at the back of a drawer, and even though I knew I wasn't allowed to, I went to the forest anyway. I hadn't been there for weeks, and as I reached it something felt different – something invisible that made the air feel thin and empty.

As I'd leant against Mami in the wardrobe and felt her warm tears against my face, I had finally realized who the glass eye belonged to, I'd realized what Ali had lost in the forest. He'd searched but couldn't find it because I already had.

It didn't take long to reach the ledge that looked over the mountainside. Ali had liked it there because he could feel the wind on his face, but now I saw why the forest felt different. Further down the slope, it had vanished. The whole bottom part of it was gone, the hillside torn up in giant bites. The trees had fallen away like blades of grass, leaving wounds of red earth and white rock. The tree with the hollow in its trunk where I'd found a broken blue eggshell, the patch of edible thistles, the old carob tree we'd set up our tent under, the hollow where lilies grew in spring, the slope where Karim had fallen and I'd picked the grit out of his knee – gone. All that was there were two big trucks, their backs piled high with rocks.

Close to the edge where you could feel the breeze, I scooped out a hole. The eye shook in my palm, then dropped into the earth. After I'd covered it, I stuck a paper windmill I'd brought with me into the ground, and the coloured wheel glistened as it turned in flashes of red and yellow. But something had changed, and as I turned back, I noticed that the cicadas had stopped singing.

Chapter Twenty-two

God was angry about Ali's death. The shelling grew much worse, bad enough for the Rose Man, Samira and Ghada to come and stay. 'It's safer here than upstairs,' Mami insisted, so the Rose Man hobbled down the steps, leaning heavily on his stick, a daughter guiding him on either side.

'Damn their souls for ruining our peace,' he mumbled. 'May they have as little rest as I, and twice as much toilet trouble.'

'Half the country's living in their basements,' said Uncle Wadih. But we didn't have a basement so we sat in the corridor – Teta and Uncle, Mami and Papi, the Rose Man and his daughters, Naji and I.

Papi dragged the armchair into the corridor for the Rose Man, and Mami fetched a blanket in case he got cold. Samira fussed with it so much, pulling and tucking it round him like pastry, that he popped.

'Stop that!' he said, snatching irritably at the blanket. 'I may not be able to walk like I used to any more, but I haven't yet reached the stage where you have to lift my little finger for me.'

With a slow nod, Ghada gave Samira a just-as-I-told-you look, smiled at Uncle, then helped Mami stick candles onto saucers ready for when evening came.

Even so early in the day the wooden shutters were pulled shut so that it was as dim as a cave inside. The only light came through the mesh door in the kitchen, and from the watery bars of light in the shutter slats. Loud bangs rattled the windows, and behind that, a roaring like the sea filled the valley. Perhaps it really was the sea. Maybe the men with bombs had broken it somehow and it had started to flood, like in the Bible.

Teta and Ghada's voices blinked on and off between the bangs. They were talking about whose house in town had been hit. 'Down the road,' said Teta, 'the glass shattered and fell round them. My neighbour was telling me about it. She has a way with jasmines. I can't grow them myself, but she has the way with them.'

I played noughts and crosses, Samira flicked nervously through a magazine, Uncle sat reading a book, and Naji tried to make a sailboat out of a tin can, two twigs and an old sock. I wanted to point out that it just looked like a tin can, two twigs and a sock, but he seemed content so I didn't.

Mami had finished some mending and was organizing her sewing basket. She wound the stray ends of thread back onto their spools, then the pins and needles were stuck in, the memory buttons put away in their jar and the scraps of material tied together. The basket was closed, and the clothes put to one side.

'I'll make you children a sandwich.' But neither of us was hungry. It was Samira who was hungry.

'Bombing makes me nervous, and my nerves make me

hungry,' she explained, and got up to prepare some food. 'It'll keep my hands busy for two minutes.'

'Help yourself to whatever you want,' said Mami.

Samira obeyed. Five minutes later she came back carrying a plate piled with two sandwiches, olives, a cucumber, pickles, four little cakes and some figs.

'Are you really going to eat all that?' asked Ghada, wide-eyed. 'You don't eat that much in a week!'

'Don't embarrass us, Samira,' added the Rose Man, squinting to see what she had. When he saw, he exclaimed, '*Ya weyli* – what are you? A locust?'

Naji let out a laugh but Papi motioned him to be quiet.

'He's right. Don't eat so much, sister,' said Ghada.

'Leave me alone, will you?' Samira snapped. 'I may as well eat.'

'Yes, let the girl eat,' said Teta. 'Why shouldn't she? She needs to put some meat on her frame. And we're not strangers.'

Ghada watched each mouthful, wincing every time a shell landed, until it was all gone.

'You're the one who should eat something,' Samira told her father when she'd finished. 'Something nourishing. How do you expect to feel better when—'

'*Phhhht*,' he interrupted, getting to his feet and heading towards the bathroom. 'Stop nagging and let me go and make water fly in peace.' The door closed behind him.

'Uncle, what are you reading?'

'Just a book.'

'Is it difficult? You've been on the same page for ages. You could tell me a story instead.'

With a smile, he closed the book. 'What story do you want, *habibti*?'

A shell screeched, held its breath, then landed with a crash that made the house tremble.

I huddled closer to Uncle's stool. 'Mami says that's the worst moment: the quiet one when you don't know where it's going to land.'

We looked at her as, with a shaking hand, she picked a speck of lint off Papi's shoulder. Then she smoothed his shirt and smiled at him.

'Something from *A Thousand and One Nights*.'

After a little thought, Uncle began. It was one I didn't know about a sultan, and his brother who'd been sent away. 'And the sultan married a beautiful woman called Scheherazade. And do you know how many days and nights it took her husband to realize he loved her?'

'A thousand and one?'

Uncle nodded. 'The stories saved her life.'

'But how can a story save your life?' asked Naji. 'That's impossible.'

'Why? Stories are important. Don't you know how important they are?' Uncle carried on, telling us about the sultan's brother who gathered armies to return and fight him, but soon the shelling grew so loud that everyone stopped listening. Mami moved to sit on the floor at Papi's feet, and he twirled and twirled a loose strand of her hair round his fingers so that it made a black ring round his gold one. Ghada and Samira sat close together, Naji hugged his tin can to his chest, and no sound came out of Uncle's moving lips as he continued the story of the sultan's wife.

At about three o'clock it grew quieter, and Naji decided he wanted to make something out of *papier mâché*.

I went into the kitchen to fetch him a dish of flour and water. Teta was watching Mami grill two aubergines over a flame on the hob.

'He'll never marry,' she said, 'and those girls in there know it by now or else they're stupid. He may talk to them, and my son can talk the teeth out of a tiger's mouth.' She gave a chuckle as if this side of her boy pleased her. 'He may even kiss them and put thoughts into their heads, into any woman's, but when it comes to anything more . . .' She tipped back her head with a click of the tongue.

'But why shouldn't he marry?' asked Mami.

'Because of Yumna. I know my son. He'd have killed himself when she died.' Black specks rose like bonfire flakes from the aubergines and floated to the ceiling. 'There won't be another for him.'

Mami nodded. 'I think you're right.'

'She married a rich man for the sake of her parents and spent the rest of her life, what little there was left of it, with the corners of her mouth turned down.'

'What did she die of?' asked Mami.

'Who knows? Everyone said something different. But the poor girl was unhappy. She was unhappy so she died.'

'Was it because her husband had gold teeth?' I asked.

They looked down at me with puzzled frowns, then returned to their conversation.

'Poor woman,' whispered Mami.

Teta muttered something about blessing the dead and followed me when I took a dish of flour paste back to Naji.

'Father?' The Rose Man was pushing the living-room shutters open a little way. 'Father, what are you doing?' Ghada held up both hands like little wings.

Samira tutted. 'He's checking his roses. Don't you know your own father by now?' She grimaced. '*Ach*, my stomach.'

'Didn't I tell you? Didn't I say you shouldn't eat so much?' said Ghada.

The shutters rasped closed again and the Rose Man reappeared, hunched over his stick. 'Sometimes when I wake in the morning,' he told Teta as he sat down, 'I think I'm still a young man.' He leant his stick beside Naji's crutch. 'And then I remember. I get up, look in the mirror and see a bent old man.' He gazed curiously at his shrivelled arm.

Teta nodded. 'When I was a little girl I had more energy than an ant. We started work when the stars were still out, while my mother made *laban*. She used to make it before the sun rose. She said it tasted better that way.' Teta paused. 'Do you think we'll ever be free of the past?'

No answer came.

For half an hour, Naji slapped strips of paper onto a balloon, smoothing and patting them with cracked white fingers.

'But what's it supposed to be?' I asked.

'A pig.'

'A pig!' I looked at it from the other side. Then I narrowed my eyes.

'It *is* a pig,' said Naji.

The lampshade shook as another shell landed. 'You're right.'

'May God break their heads!' exclaimed Samira, rubbing her stomach. 'Oh, those pickles.' She groaned. 'My stomach can't take vinegar. If I live through the night, God help me, I'll never touch another pickle.'

I looked through a book of puzzles to see if there were any I hadn't done yet, but there weren't. Then a loud pop made Samira jump.

'In God's name!' Ghada's hand went to her heart.

'Naji!'

There was a resettling in chairs.

'You popped it too soon,' I said. The newspaper was sunk and floppy in the middle. 'It looks like . . .' But it didn't look like anything.

By the time darkness fell, the shelling was even worse. The walls and furniture were old friends now: the crack running the length of the corridor and down one wall, the hole in the low chair big enough to poke a finger through, the loose bathroom door-handle, the fingerprints on the bathroom window-ledge where I climbed up to see outside.

'The house is going to collapse on our heads,' I said to Naji as everything shook again.

If it did fall, we'd be squashed under the stone that made up the Rose Man's flat and everything in it: his bed and wardrobe, his sink and bathtub, his carpets and books.

Although it had grown dark, no one lit any candles. Samira had the bowl of sweets Mami kept for visitors in her lap and was eating them.

'I saw half a jar of pickles still left in the kitchen,' said Ghada sharply. 'Do you want me to fetch them for you?'

But Samira just carried on eating.

Uncle had his book open again but the pages still weren't turning. Papi and the Rose Man had been listening to the radio that stood between them, but now Papi turned it off.

Clicking sounds came from the Rose Man's mouth as he settled his false teeth. 'So this is what we get for Hitler's insanity.'

Mami looked up. 'What?'

'War is a circle, like the seasons. Without the First World War there would have been no Second World War, and that crazy man would have stayed on the streets and died a lunatic as he deserved to. But instead his victims are still running round the same track, and now it's us and the Palestinians who've become dirty Arabs and less-than-humans.'

'It's not the same thing, Father,' huffed Ghada.

The Rose Man exploded: 'Not the same thing? Don't you know what they've been doing down in Beirut the last two days? Our soldiers, *ours*, have been butchering hundreds, maybe thousands of Palestinians in Shatila and Sabra – women and children, lining them up beside mass graves and packing them in.'

Papi dragged his hands over his face. 'They must have been drugged so they could do it – they must have been! How else do you get a man to kill babies?'

'They've all done unspeakable things, drugged or not,' said the Rose Man. 'They've done those things because evil is here.' He struck his chest.

Now Uncle spoke, his voice low. 'They're saying that the Israeli forces sealed the camps and watched. Lit flares for the soldiers to do their work, and said the people in those camps were terrorists.'

'And that son of thieves Begin sits there talking about the invasion of Beirut and the Holocaust in the same breath,' the Rose Man added. 'They're animals, all of them – both sides, all sides! Ours, theirs, all of them!'

Papi bit his finger. 'You're right,' he said. 'You're right. We're all the same.'

Getting up quickly, Mami brought candles. The bright circles wavered and wobbled as she set them down. Their light turned table, chairs and faces watery, and nothing felt real.

Papi spoke slowly. 'I have nothing against anyone any longer. Jews or Palestinians, we're born what we're born. It's the things we do afterwards that count.'

The Rose Man stopped plucking his blanket, his eyes glittering in the darkness. 'There we're agreed. Some men have war in their hearts. But war isn't only in the soldier's heart, Nabeel. That's what most people don't see. It's in the heart of the man in the suit – the man with the fat wallet, the smiling mouth and the sweet tongue – in his heart maybe most of all. Perhaps he pulls more triggers than anyone, even though his finger never once touches a gun.'

In the silences between blasts, the clock ticked on, and Mami peeled apples that no one ate. The one in her hand turned round and round, the red peel not breaking till the whole fruit was white. When it was done she put it on the plate, took up another and began peeling again.

A shell wailed and everyone paused to hear where it would land. Then the earth shook, and the sound of breaking glass came from the living room.

'The window,' moaned Ghada, biting her lip.

An apple skin broke, fell half on and half off Mami's lap and hung there, a short coil of flecked red, while on the floor at her feet, the plate of naked white apples had begun to turn brown.

'Did I tell you, Aida, what to do with that cutting?' asked Teta suddenly. 'You . . . you have to wait till it gets roots before you can plant it. Put it in water, that's all. In water. Then give it some good earth.'

Mami's face was pale as she laid down her knife.

'Be gentle when you plant it. And it'll like the sun.'

When another loud blast came, Mami clutched Papi's arm and laid her head on his shoulder. No one was doing anything now. Inside the house there was silence, except for the squeaks or mutters or prayers or curses each time a shell landed.

I covered my eyes and tried to picture the forest. It would be quiet there. The trees kept everything out, even the bombs, even the sound. It was still hot as midsummer there. The trees and bushes were humming and chirping, the birds hopping in the branches high overhead. Under low leaves, woodlice and small centipedes were curled up, while earwigs and ants scuttled left and right across the red earth. Strange flowers were opening, and red and black butterflies floated and bobbed on the air. I walked down the worn paths again, touching the tree bark and tall grasses covered with bubbles that donkeys must have spat as they passed. The sticky green smell of pine cones was everywhere, and soon the dry brown pods hanging from the old carob tree would start to stink. The pine needles crunched under my feet; an empty cone dried out by the heat crackled as I trod on it. The trees were warm with sun and the yellow sap that flowed beneath their flaky skins, and the forest was alive.

There was another crash close by and shrapnel tinkled on the veranda. I took my hands from my eyes. It was dark and the forest was gone. At the bottom of the slope, I knew that few trees were left, and that soon they would be gone as well.

The Rose Man's yellow socks glowed pale beneath his trouser hems. 'What do you think?' he asked Papi. 'Where are they shelling from?'

'They'll be shooting from the mountains to the east across the valley, right across to the high road.'

Samira had just asked Teta something, but Teta ignored it. 'The high road?'

'Yes.'

'My friend lives on the high road. You know Latifeh, the one from all those years back, from Africa?' In the dim candlelight, she glanced at Uncle Wadih.

'That's life here.' Papi sighed. 'You live or die by where the architect chose to lay the first stone.'

I got up and went to him. 'But Papi, Amal lives there too. I visited and we played on the veranda. We could see right down into the valley.' I touched his arm. 'Is it bad to be where they are?'

'Yes, even more dangerous than here.'

'Can't we go and get them? They can stay with us.'

'You want the whole world to spend the war in our corridor?'

'I'll come with you, Papi,' said Naji, struggling to get up. 'I want to come with you. Look, I can lean on my foot now, see?' He put some weight on the bandaged leg. 'I can even walk on it. I can!'

'Sit down, son. I know you'll walk on it again, but not tonight.'

Uncle Wadih ground his teeth as Teta lamented, '*Ya haram.* They'll be killed in their beds. They'll be killed, and the little child . . .'

Papi got up, paced about, then sat down again.

'Wadih,' said Teta, 'go and get them. You never even paid your respects after she died.'

The teeth-grinding stopped. 'You want me to go and pay my respects now, fifteen years later and under the flying shells?' he barked.

Papi stood up again. He patted Uncle's shoulder, then walked up and down the corridor and round his and Mami's bedroom twice, running his hand through his hair so that it stood up.

'Wadih,' came Teta's voice again, 'go and get them, my son, before it's too late. I know she's not your daughter, but she might have been. Don't you care?'

Ghada and Samira waited for his answer.

'My life is cheap!' he shouted. 'I have no family, no wife or children, and that old woman's the reason why!'

'She's not the same woman as then. She's sick. She barely even remembers you.'

'Not remember that she wouldn't let me marry her daughter?' He waved his arm. 'She smashed up my life, and now you want me to go and get blown up with her!'

The old woman *had* put a curse on one of Teta's sons. It was Uncle's life she had ruined.

'I'm going to get them.' It was Papi. He'd stopped pacing. A fine spray of sweat stood out on his forehead, and his shirt was dotted with it. 'I don't want anyone else to step out of this house. I'm going to get them.'

Chapter Twenty-three

No one told Papi not to go. For a brief moment it looked as though Uncle would offer to fetch them instead, but then he leant back again, saying nothing.

Samira fiddled with the skin on her neck, then turned to Mami. 'Let's go and do something. We'll prepare some food for when they get back. Aida?' She laid a hand on Mami's arm, but Mami didn't notice. She took two steps across to Papi and put her arms round his neck.

Naji watched, his top teeth over his bottom lip. Another piece of glass fell from the living-room window to the floor, but Teta was smiling. When Papi went to the bedroom for his car keys, Mami followed, and there was murmuring and the sound of kisses.

As I passed Teta on the way to Naji's bedroom, she was praying with her eyes tight shut and her hands clasped together. A few moments later I reached for the window-frame and pulled myself up. It was easier this time: the drawers seemed big and firm as stairs. Then I was up. Remembering how the wall had scraped my legs the last time, I jumped down. I was going with Papi. Amal wouldn't come with him otherwise. I knew she wouldn't.

Papi hadn't come out yet, and the car was in its usual place opposite the rubbish bins. From there, a cat, its eyes two pinpricks of light, watched me open the back door of the car. I climbed in and lay on the floor to wait. The torn rubber mat felt horribly ridged, and a little stone dug into my knee. Underneath the front seat was a lollipop covered in fluff.

I counted to thirty but still Papi didn't come.

The scream of a shell cut through the air, and the ground shivered with a boom as an explosion hit. I moved the small stone from under my knee and tossed it to the other side of the car. Amal would be scared by the noise. In some corner of that empty, echoing house she would be squatting, round and silent as a fruit. The old woman would be shaking, except no one would be able to tell whether or not it was from fear.

Another mortar shell passed overhead with a yowl. I sat up and peered out of the window. The house was shuttered. Only a dim light came through the kitchen door.

A car's headlights glimmered on the railings and, sinking back down, I started to count again. I'd only reached nine when the house door banged and footsteps hurried towards the car. The door creaked and Papi got in. A lump appeared in the back of the driver's seat. Then there was a jangling of keys and a cough as the engine half caught. Papi tried again, but it wasn't until the fourth time that the motor whirred into life.

Above us, the sky lit up and there was a thud. 'God save us,' Papi muttered as he put the car into gear, the back of his head glinting in the light of a rising moon.

With a heave, we screeched and clacked out into the road. I slid right then left again as Papi straightened the car, rolling against the rear seats as we pulled up the hill. I knew the way to the high road, but couldn't keep up with the bumps and braking, the swinging from side to side as we swerved round corners. There was no muttering or cursing or sighing from the front seat, but outside the breaking up of Ein Douwra grew louder.

We were on the high road now: there was the tree with the cardboard sign on its branch.

Just then a wail split the sky. Something big landed close by with a crash and stuff clinked on the car bonnet like rain. With a great jolt, we went into a pothole and my arm smashed into the handle that wound the window up and down.

'*Aiyyy!*'

Papi's head jerked, the car pulled out of the hole and I slammed into the door again.

'Ruba?'

The car was still moving. As he drove, Papi kept glancing over his shoulder, then back at the road. He let out a moan when he saw it was me.

'Stop – I want to get up!' I struggled to climb onto the seat. 'Stop a minute!'

'I can't. Stay where you are.'

We drove on, until finally the car slowed down. Pebbles crunched beneath the tyres as we left the road and pulled into the old woman's yard. Then with a lurch and a grind of the handbrake, we stopped.

Papi's door opened and he got out.

'Wait for me!' My fingers were slipping on the catch but he was already half running towards the house. 'Wait!'

He stopped, looked at the house, then back at me as I fumbled with the catch. When my door swung open he was still standing undecided next to the grey shape of the fountain. Low in the sky, a round moon glowed clean white. Then with a sudden rush, Papi was back and took me up in his arms. 'I can walk – put me down! I'm too old to be carried,' but he didn't seem to hear. He felt hot as an oven as I jolted and bounced in his arms – across the yard, past the fountain, past the two big trees with rustly leaves and the smaller mulberry tree, past the chicken coop that I'd opened.

When we reached the front door, I slid to the ground, leaving Papi's shirtfront sticking to him. He knocked on the doorframe. No one came so he banged this time, louder.

'It's Nabeel Khouri! Can you hear me? Nabeel Khouri! I've come to take you to our house.' Something wailed across the sky, followed by a fast crackle of gunfire. 'My mother sent me. It's safer in our house.'

Behind the mesh door a shape moved. Then the door opened and she was looking at us. The dark eyes moved slowly from me to Papi, and she smiled. '*Ahlan.*' A hand waved us calmly inside. 'Come in, come in.'

'My mother sent me,' repeated Papi. 'You and your girl must come to our house. It's not far. It will be safer there.'

But the old woman only stepped to one side for us to go in. I looked back towards the car. The lump of the fountain was still there, pale in the moonlight, and I wondered how long ago it had stopped spouting water.

The only light in the house came from the next room.

'Do you want to bring anything with you?' Papi asked. 'What shall I get for you?'

'I'm going to find Amal,' I told Papi.

The roaring grew louder as I crossed the kitchen. Through the window, I saw the sky light up in fits and scribbles, making the sort of noise Naji said was anti-aircraft fire. Perhaps the valley would crack open soon and suck us all in.

Two candles stood on the dresser. Still there, the stack of plates I'd seen before, the table and four wooden chairs, the sofa with the blue cotton sheet over it, the bare tiles.

She was sitting cross-legged on the floor in front of the sofa. The edge of the blue sheet had been raised and lay on top of her head, covering her hair and eyes. She held her doll in her lap.

'Amal!'

She didn't move.

I went up close. 'Amal! My father's come to take you to our house.' I lifted the sheet up. Her large eyes were open, but there was no surprise, no fear, nothing at all. 'You can bring your doll.'

She looked down at it and smoothed the wiry hair.

'*Yalla*, Amal. Don't you want to come to my house? You haven't been there yet.'

She stroked the doll's cheek now, touched its mouth.

Amal's grandmother came in. Papi came after, dabbing the sides of his face with his sleeve. He looked round the room, then out of the window towards the valley.

The old woman laid a hand on Amal's head. I felt the weight of her body beside me, heavy as flour, felt the sandy-rough breath grating out of her chest. The shivering hand on Amal's head made her look up. 'You'll go with them. It's better there. Quieter.'

Amal didn't move. Her eyes were fixed on her grandmother, but the old woman turned to Papi. 'Here, take this for her.'

229

She passed him a plastic bag wrapped round something small. '*Yalla*, Amal, *yalla*, my life.'

Slowly, Amal got to her feet.

'Are you hungry? Shall I fry you some eggs before you go?'

Papi ran a hand through his hair. 'You're coming too,' he said, but the old woman only laughed, tipping back her head.

'I'm not going anywhere.' She clicked her tongue. 'Where would you have me go? I know every stone in my house, and the spaces in between those stones.'

'We haven't got time to discuss such things now. Hurry, bring what you need and come.'

The old woman's breasts shuddered with laughter. 'And who'll take care of them all? The house, the fountain, the garden, my husband. Who is there to take care of them but me?'

The plates in the dresser rattled as a shell dropped, but Papi was staring wide-eyed at the old woman. We followed her into the kitchen, where she opened a cupboard and moved some bags and tins to one side.

'I've got some *kishk* somewhere in here. Why don't you take some with you? For the children. Don't you hear what a noise they're making outside?' She chuckled. 'Always shouting and playing and making a din.' She found the jar, pulled it out and turned to Papi with a smile. 'This batch is made from special yoghurt, yoghurt I made myself. I ground it up fine as dust. I had to get a net to put over it when it was drying – I sent for it specially – to stop the flies getting at it. And when you come to cook it, take . . . Well, you know how to make *kishk*. There's nothing to it.'

She held out the jar and Papi took it. He pulled me out onto the doorstep. But Amal had come alive now. She clung to her grandmother's apron, her face pressed to the round stomach.

There were comforting noises, and the wrinkled old hands shivered and shook as they cupped themselves round Amal's head. 'Don't be a nuisance now. Don't trouble the man. I'll come and find you tomorrow.'

Papi touched the old woman's arm, and there was pity in his voice now. 'Come with us and see to her. She hasn't anyone but you. Don't you see she wants you?'

Two huge bangs from the valley made Amal cling to the apron.

'No. God will look after me here. He'll send me what He sends me.'

Papi's voice rose. 'But this is no punishment! This is a war!'

'A war,' she repeated. An instant later she swatted away the crackle of gunfire. 'No. Don't you hear the children playing outside? I'm not going anywhere.'

'Please.' A bead of sweat dripped down Papi's temple. 'Stop making it so difficult for me.'

With her hands still clasped round Amal's head, the old woman gave a little jolt and seemed to remember something. 'Is that you? Have you come back?' She beamed. 'You've come again to ask if you can have my girl, haven't you?'

Papi breathed in sharply. Another explosion shook the pots and chairs, and there was a sound of something breaking at the back of the house.

I spoke up. 'No, this isn't Uncle Wadih.'

Papi stood holding the jar of *kishk*. 'I'm not Wadih.'

Amal's grandmother laughed as if this was a good joke. She let out a long sigh. 'Don't worry, my boy, don't worry. This time I'm going to say yes.' She stroked Amal's hair and turned her to face us. 'Here, take her. Isn't she beautiful? Isn't she? My beautiful, beautiful daughter.' She bent to kiss Amal's head. 'No, don't look like that, my son. It's a man's duty to smile, so smile.'

The old woman moved out onto the doorstep with us. She was close to me now, close and warm, and something made me take her hand in both of mine. I felt it all over – the rough hardened palm, the creases at every finger joint, the ridged nails, and then the back of it, soft and crinkled as the skin on boiled milk. 'Come with us. Please.'

But she only smiled and stroked my cheek.

The sky flared like lightning, and there was a string of bangs. Holding the door open, the old woman gave a little laugh and shook her head. 'Are they letting off fireworks again?' she said. Then she peered anxiously at Papi. 'You look tired. Go home and rest. Get my girl to make you some *kishk*. And pick some marigolds to take with you before winter comes. My Yumna loves marigolds.'

We stumbled across the dark yard. The moon had moved behind the trees and glimmered through the leaves in white splinters.

'It's turned her head,' muttered Papi. 'This war has turned her head.'

Amal stopped to look back and I did too, but her grandmother was facing away from us.

'Doesn't she know her daughter's dead?' I asked Papi. 'Let me go back and tell her.'

'There's no point. It would make no difference.' Then, still clutching the jar and the small plastic bag the old woman had given him, he steered Amal towards the car.

The last time I looked back, the old woman was standing in the doorway staring after us, and as I looked she smiled, showing big teeth. She smiled and smiled until she had a lip from ear to ear. And above and all around her, the sky flashed bright.

'Ruba!' cried Mami when we got back.

Teta crossed herself, and Uncle, who had stood up suddenly, sank back into his chair.

'Where were you?' asked Naji, leaning on his crutches.

Mami took hold of me, her nails digging into my shoulders. Then her arms were wrapped tight round me. The thin blue shirt smelt of spring flowers, and beneath that, the faint sour smell that was her. Her arms stayed round me, her chest moving quickly in and out, in and out, her black-fringed eyes squeezed shut.

Then I was passed to Teta for the same treatment. Between hugs, I saw that the ends of Ghada's hair on one side were damp with chewing, and that the sweet bowl beside Samira was now empty. Sitting in the ripples and furls of candlelight, the Rose Man was making wet noises as he moved his teeth about in his mouth.

Two explosions, one after the other, shook the walls and sent us back into the darkened corridor.

All evening the shells wailed and fell, and the earth shivered, but there was nowhere else to hide. When Papi told her about her friend, Teta moaned and cried, gently slapping her thighs.

'She was . . .' Papi couldn't finish. He picked me up, and from the hard way he was holding me, I thought he was going to run somewhere. But then his body went soft and

233

he put me down. He was staring at Amal. She sat curled on the floor beside his chair tugging at her socks and looking at the ceiling each time a bomb landed as though it would crack like an eggshell.

The candles burnt low. One went out but no one bothered to light another in its place. There was nothing but deep growls and blasts outside, and inside, a silence speckled with soft prayers.

When Amal began to cry no one went to her. Either they didn't notice because she made no noise, or there was nothing they could do about it. Uncle had lit a cigarette and was using the empty sweet bowl as an ashtray, and Papi was gazing steadily at one spot on the floor.

'What's going to happen, Mami?' I asked.

It was a long time before she answered. 'I don't know, my love. I don't know.'

Amal reached up towards Papi's sleeve. Her touch seemed to wake him. They stayed looking at each other a long time, his face turned down and hers turned up, until suddenly he leant over and lifted her onto his chair.

She gripped the white cotton of his shirt sleeve as she settled down, then fell asleep stretched across the chair from armrest to armrest with Papi trapped underneath.

Huddled on two cushions on the floor, I must have slept too, because when I opened my eyes again another candle had burnt out, and the bangs from outside had moved away a little. Uncle Wadih and the Rose Man were trying to rest in their chairs. Ghada and Samira, covered with a blanket, lay close together on a mattress someone had dragged into the corridor, while Teta and Naji slept on another just inside the dining room.

Mami was lifting Amal off Papi's chair. When he stood up, she laid Amal back again. With a grimace, Papi stretched and followed Mami into the kitchen. My eyelids were heavy but I didn't want to sleep, and went and stood in the kitchen doorway.

Mami was kissing Papi's cheek. 'Eat something, Nabeel. You haven't eaten since yesterday.'

He held her face in both hands and planted four kisses on it, one on the forehead, one on each cheek and the last on her mouth. 'I'm not hungry.'

'Why did she give you *kishk*?'

Papi half smiled. 'The girl comes complete with a jarful of dust.'

The small plastic bag the old woman had given him for Amal was on the counter. He picked it up now and opened it. There was nothing inside but a little wad of money and a limp sandwich.

'No, I'm not hungry,' he said again. 'Only thirsty.'

It was true, because, grabbing the glass water-jug from the shelf, he tilted back his head and poured water into his mouth from above so that it came out of the spout in a constant stream. His mouth stayed open for a long time, his throat-bone moving in and out as he swallowed. Naji had been practising swallowing open-mouthed like that for a year but still couldn't do it.

Papi drank till the jug was empty, then refilled it and carried it back into the corridor. I woke many times in the night and always found Papi drinking. He drank like a man who'd been lost in the desert. With his mouth open like a lion's, the glistening water-stream made a solid silver arch into his throat. And each time he drank till the jug was empty.

The last time I woke he was leaning over Amal, gazing into her face. Everyone was asleep. Naji had one arm thrown out over his head, and was still wearing one shoe. The Rose Man was snoring. But Papi had seen me, and came towards me like a ghost.

Squatting, he stroked a strand of hair off my face; and even when it was gone he carried on stroking. It was a long time before he stopped. I touched his hand and it was warm and soft, the knuckles no longer like pebbles but flesh and bone, each one round and good and comforting. And as he bent to kiss me in the dim light, I thought that the stain mark on his forehead was paler, as though it had been washed away. When he stood up again he was smiling, and it was like a gift, that smile. It had no sadness or disappointment in it.

As I burrowed into the quiet place where the wall met the floor, I had one last thought: I was glad he'd drunk all that water, and that he was no longer a cactus standing motionless in a pot full of dry cracked earth.

Acknowledgments

With thanks to Eva Lewin, Stef Pixner, Jenny Downham,
Spike Warwick, and Steve Cook. Also to Matthew Martin,
without whose loving support and encouragement
I would not be a writer.